AVA and TACO CAT

"Bold, funny, and real."
– Karen Bokram, editor of *Girls' Life* magazine, on *Ava XOX*

PRAISE FOR *AVA AND PIP*

"Through Ava's diary entries, Weston perfectly captures the complexities of sisterhood...a love letter to language."

—*The New York Times Book Review*

"Ava Wren makes reading and writing so much fun, she deserves a T-O-P-S-P-O-T on your bookshelf. This charming diary will inspire shy kids, young writers, and even reluctant readers. Y-A-Y for A-V-A!"

—Dan Greenburg, author of The Zack Files series

"With her engaging voice, jaw-dropping wordplay, and tales of good people making not-so-good decisions, she casts the perfect spell. A big W-O-W for *Ava and Pip*!"

—Julie Sternberg, author of *Like Pickle Juice on a Cookie*

"Will have readers cheering."

—*Booklist*

"Just enough conflict to keep the pages flying, with the comfortable certainty that it will all work out."

—*School Library Journal*

"You're gonna fall head over heels for the new book by our very own advice columnist Carol Weston."

—*Girls' Life*

"The charming story covers writing, sisterhood, and events that occasionally, says Ava, are 'making me feel like P-O-O-P.'"

—*Yale Magazine*

"Weston deals with family dynamics and creative challenges in realistic, emotionally honest ways."

—*Shelf Awareness*

"A witty, warm, wonderful story... As with all good books, I was both eager to find out, and reluctant to have it over, noting with sorrow the dwindling pages."

—Neil Steinberg, columnist at the *Chicago Sun-Times*

"Young readers will be enchanted with this endearing story about two very different sisters and their journey to find their voices."

—*Pittsburgh Post-Gazette*

"Such a wonderful book. It's so gratifying to see a child devour a book."

—Laura Ingraham

"Filled with funny wordplay, this clever story will grab anyone who has ever felt overlooked."

—*Discovery Girls*

"YAY!"

—Jon Agee, author of *The Incredible Painting of Felix Clousseau* and *Go Hang a Salami! I'm a Lasagna Hog!*

AVA

and

TACO CAT

BY

CAROL WESTON

Published by Sourcebooks Jabberwocky, an imprint of Sourcebooks, Inc.
P.O. Box 4410, Naperville, Illinois 60567-4410
(630) 961-3900
Fax: (630) 961-2168
www.sourcebooks.com

The Library of Congress has cataloged the hardcover edition as follows:

Weston, Carol.
Ava and Taco Cat / Carol Weston.
pages cm
Summary: Fifth-grader Ava writes in her diary about her family, losing her best friend to a new girl, and adopting an injured, skittish, and very special cat.
(13 : alk. paper) [1. Cats--Fiction. 2. Family life--Fiction. 3. Friendship--Fiction. 4. Diaries--Fiction.] I. Title.
PZ7.W526285Ax 2015
[Fic]--dc23

2014039773

Source of Production: Versa Press, East Peoria, Illinois, USA
Date of Production: January 2016
Run Number: 5005635

Printed and bound in the United States of America
VP 10 9 8 7 6 5 4 3 2 1

To the cats in my life,
cuddly and otherwise:
Rosie,
Smokey,
Pokey,
Lilac,
Chanda,
Slate,
and
Mike

12/28

Dear Brand-New Diary,

I'm really worried. At dinner tonight, Mom said that right before closing, a man came into the clinic with an injured cat. He'd found him shivering in a tree! The cat was scrawny and scared and his neck had a gash and his left ear was bitten up. The man got the cat down and took him to the nearest vet—which was Dr. Gross.

"Poor cat!" I said.

"Is he going to be okay?" Pip asked.

"I don't know," Mom said. "Dr. Gross stitched him up and gave him antibiotics. If he makes it through the night, we'll call the shelter in the morning."

"*If!?*" I said.

Mom nodded. "I think a coyote got to him."

"What's his name?" Pip asked.

"No idea. But he's neutered, so he's not feral." Pip and I know that "feral" means wild, and "neutered" means he can't make baby cats. But does Mom know that stories about hurt cats and dogs make me sad?

"What does he look like?" I asked.

"He's honey-colored," Mom said. "But his right leg and paw are white, and he has a white zigzag above his nose."

"Awww," I said, trying to picture the cat's sweet little zigzag.

"No chip or collar or anything?" Dad said.

"No identification at all," Mom said.

Soon Mom and Dad and Pip were talking about other things, including dinner, which was stuffed eggplant—*blecch*! (Dad just started a terrible tradition of "Meatless Mondays." Fortunately, tonight he also made plain bow tie noodles for me.)

Well, I couldn't stop thinking about how lonely that cat probably felt all by himself in a cage at Dr. Gross's. I wished we could go check on him. But no way would Mom agree to go back to work after she'd already come home and put on her slippers.

I was trying to imagine what it must have been like for the skinny cat when the coyote started attacking him. He must have known it was life or death. He probably thought he was a goner for sure! It was lucky he was able to scamper up that tree, but then he must have been too afraid to come back down! And maybe too weak? I bet he was starving as well as stuck and petrified! Poor little thing!!

Suddenly my nose and eyes started tingling. I blurted, "May I be excused?" but it was too late! Teardrops fell right onto my bow tie noodles.

"Are you *crying*?" Pip asked, surprised.

"Oh, Ava." Mom met my eyes. "I'm sorry I brought it up."

Dad gave my hand a squeeze, and I ran upstairs and splashed

water on my face. I don't know why I was getting so upset about a lost honey-colored cat. But I was. I *am*.

It's just so sad to think of him all alone in a cage instead of a home.

AVA, UPSET

12/28
A LITTLE LATER

DEAR DIARY,

After dinner, Pip came and knocked on my door, which was nice of her. She's been easier to talk to now that she's an official teenager. I think it's because she's been coming out of her shell instead of staying scrunched up inside it.

Anyway, she said, "Want to do another page?" so I said sure. Pip and I started making a book on the third day of winter break when we both got bored at the exact same time. I'm the author and Pip is the illustrator.

I'd wanted us to write *A Duck Out of Luck*, but I couldn't come up with a plot. Then I suggested *A Goose on the Loose*, but I couldn't come up with a plot for that either. Finally we decided to make an alphabet book because alphabet books don't have plots. I said it could be about animals, but Pip said it should be about fish.

Pip is constantly doodling fish. Her favorite stuffed animal is an orange fish named Otto. She named it Otto for two reasons:

1. O-T-T-O is a palindrome. It's spelled the same backward and forward, like A-V-A and P-I-P and M-O-M and D-A-D.

2. Otto is the name of the fish in *A Fish Out of Water*, which was the first book Pip read all by herself. (She has now read about a bazillion books.)

So far, our book is two pages long. It's called *Alphabet Fish*, and these are the two pages:

A is for angelfish.

The shy little angelfish has fins like wings.
Shh! It is hiding among weeds, rocks, and things.

and

B is for bumblebee fish.

If you found this fish, would you name it Bumblebee?
It doesn't buzz or sting, but it's black and gold, you see.

Pip has already made a list of the twenty-six fish she wants us to do. C was supposed to be for clown fish, but I thought about the lonely injured cat and said, "C should be for catfish." Pip agreed and drew a cute catfish with pointy whiskers.

I'm going to sleep now. I hope the lost cat is already asleep. What I really hope is that he makes it through the night!

Ava...Almost...Asleep

P.S. If I cross my fingers for luck, will they stay crossed while I'm asleep?

12/29
MORNING

DEAR DIARY,

In three days, I turn eleven. If I could ask for any present in the whole wide world, I would ask for a pet. But a real pet this time—one with fur.

Whenever I beg for a cat or a dog or even just a gerbil, Mom always says she has enough pets to worry about. She once admitted that the main reason she applied for her job as office manager for Dr. Gross was because the clinic is near our house—*not* because she adores animals.

I can't believe I've been alive for over a decade and have never had a real pet. I've never even had a bunny! Or a turtle! Or a frog!

The only pet Pip and I ever had was a goldfish named Goldy Lox, and we loved her, but she was not exactly Little Miss Personality. (I'm not even sure she was a she!)

Maybelle once had a frog. And last Christmas, she got one of those kits of chrysalides that turn into butterflies. This year, she got a makeup set, a manicure set, and beads for making bracelets. I don't get why so many girls in our class (including my BFF!) all of a sudden want to wear makeup, nail polish, and jewelry.

Maybelle even got a *sports bra* for Christmas. When she showed it to me, I almost fainted on the floor. But I tried to act like it was no big deal.

Later when I told Pip about Maybelle's sports bra, I pointed out that boob (B-O-O-B) is a palindrome and that bras seem like booby traps. I also mentioned that "booby trap" spelled backward is "party boob." Pip said I was being an immature idiot.

Pip thinks she's very mature because she is in seventh grade (I'm in fifth), and she has a boyfriend, Ben. He's our friend Bea's brother, and right now Bea and Ben are both in Chicago.

Our family is not going away on vacation. Mom says we're having a "staycation" in Misty Oaks.

I think "staycation" is a dumb word.

The reason we're not going anywhere is because we don't have a lot of extra money.

We aren't rich, but Mom and Dad say it's better to be *enriched*. That's why Pip takes art classes.

Mom and Dad have offered me writing classes, but I'd rather write just in you, my diary, because then I can write down all my secrets and private thoughts, and no one but me ever reads them.

So far in my life, I have started eight diaries and finished one. The one I finished last week is on my bookshelf. The other six are in my dead diary graveyard, underneath my underwear.

Here is a private thought: I *still* feel bad about what happened to Goldy Lox. Two years ago, I did not take good care of her. I accidentally overfed her, and she did not grow bigger and bigger like Otto in the picture book. She floated to the top, sideways and dead. I wanted to give her a proper burial, but Mom flushed her down the toilet. When I started to cry, she said, "Oh, Ava, it's only a fish." Which was true.

But she was *our* fish.

Ava Elle Wren, Still Just Ten

12/29
AFTER BREAKFAST

DEAR DIARY,

Outside, some of the trees have snow on their branches.

Inside, Dad made snowman pancakes just for me. That's when he places three round pancakes in a line (not a stack) and adds chocolate chip eyes to the top one.

"Can you make me a cat pancake?" I asked.

"I can try," he said, and he did try, but the tail and legs blobbed together, and the pancake looked more like an amoeba than a cat.

I said, "Do you know the Aesop fable 'The Cat and the Fox'?" Dad knows I like to read short fables more than long books, probably because (1) they are about animals, and (2) they give you a lot to think about in just a few pages.

He said, "Remind me." So I did. I said:

A fox is bragging to a cat that he knows a ton of ways to save himself from hounds. The cat says he knows only one and asks the fox to show him more. The fox sticks his snout in the air and says, "Maybe someday if I'm not toooo busy." Just then, a pack of hungry hounds comes bounding toward them, barking furiously. The cat escapes by racing up a tree and says, "This is my one and only trick. Which of yours are you going to use?" But while the fox is thinking and thinking, the hounds attack.

Dad asked what the moral was. I said: "It's good to have a plan." Then I confessed that I was still worrying about the honey-colored cat who escaped up the tree, and I wished I had a plan.

When Mom came downstairs, I asked her if she'd called Dr. Gross.

"Ava, he's not in at this hour," Mom said. "And I haven't even had my coffee yet."

Dad handed Mom a mug of coffee and mumbled, "You think the cat will have to be put down?"

Hello! I know what "put down" means! It's a euphemism for "kill"! (I know what *euphemism* means too. It's a nice way of saying something not nice. It's also an extremely advanced spelling word.)

"Depends on his condition," Mom said.

I stood up so fast, my chair fell over. "You can't kill him!" I said.

"Sweetie," Mom replied, "Dr. Gross is not in the business of killing animals. He does everything he can to *save* animals. But if the cat isn't going to get better..."

"Please don't kill him!" I felt like Fern in *Charlotte's Web* when she tells her father not to kill the runty newborn piglet. (Note: Mr. and Mrs. Arable love their daughter Fern very much, so they let her keep the piglet, and she names him Wilbur.)

"I'll call you when I get to work," Mom said. "And now I'd like to change the subject. Have you thought about what you want for your birthday?"

Without missing a beat, I said, "Yes. I want a cat. I want *that* cat!"

A-V-A Who Wants a C A T

12/29
11:40 A.M.

Dear Diary,

Mom didn't call, and when I couldn't stand it anymore, I called her even though she doesn't like to be "interrupted" at work.

"Did he make it through the night?" I asked.

"Yes, he did. He's a tough old boy."

"Can I visit him?" I could feel my heart beating extra fast.

"Actually, the man from the shelter just came and picked him up."

"*No!*"

"Ava, that's *good* news. They'll try to find a home for him."

"I want him to live in *our* home! And not all cats get adopted! You always say people like kittens best—and he's a scratched-up grown-up with ears that don't match."

"Honey, we've been through this. At the end of a long day, the last thing I want to do is deal with pets."

"It's *pet,* not pets! Singular, not plural. And you won't have to. *I'll* do everything! Besides, dogs need to be walked, but cats just sit around purring all day."

"Ava, it's a moot point, so you might as well save your breath.

That cat's been stitched up and sent on his way. He's not here anymore. I'm sorry."

"Where is he?"

"At the rescue center."

"What 'rescue center'?"

"I have to get back to work now," Mom said, sounding exasperated. But she didn't get that *I* was exasperated too!

We hung up, and I looked up "rescue center" on Dad's computer. Guess what? The Misty Oaks Rescue Center is pretty close to Taco Time, our favorite place for lunch!

Ten minutes ago, one of Dad's students showed up. Besides writing plays, Dad tutors reading and writing and helps high school seniors with their college essays. When the teenager rang the doorbell, Pip was coming downstairs. She had slept right through breakfast, which she never used to do. I decided to ask Dad if he'd give us money for lunch.

Dad said okay because he likes having a "quiet house," which is "impossible" when we are "underfoot."

Pip is now zipping up her winter boots. Here's what she and Dad don't know: I have a plan. A BIG one!

AVA ON A MISSION

12/29
3:33 (A NUMBER PALINDROME!)

DEAR DIARY,

Pip and I went to the rescue center! It's a brick building with an old bike stand near the entrance.

We parked our bikes, and I almost stepped in something warm and brown and gooshy. I told Pip to be careful, and she looked down and said, "Dog doo? Good God!" (D-O-G-D-O-O-G-O-O-D-G-O-D). That made us both crack up because "Dog doo? Good God!" is an extremely funny palindrome.

Inside, behind a counter, a lady with a high ponytail told us that if we wanted to visit the cats, we had to be accompanied by someone at least eighteen. She looked like she was around eighteen herself! Pip got nervous and whispered, "We should leave," but I convinced her to stay so that we could people-watch—and animal-watch!

I wanted to know why someone lucky enough to have a pet would decide to give him or her up. Pip and I sat down and started observing, and soon we had answers.

- A man in a suit came in with a barky dachshund and said

he and his wife had a newborn baby and couldn't keep their noisy dog.

- A woman with dark purple fingernails came in with a pit bull with claws painted the same color and said her new landlord had a "no dogs policy."
- A hippie-ish couple came in with five black-and-white kittens and said their tuxedo cat had seven kittens and they could keep only two.
- A boy and his mom came in with a bunny they called Peter Rabbit, and the mom said the boy turned out to be allergic, and the boy said, "And, it poops all over the place."

It was sad, really. All these people coming in with furry animals and leaving with empty pet carriers and droopy leashes.

Next thing you know, a family with four kids showed up and said they wanted to "pick out a dog."

Ponytail Lady left to take a lunch break, and a bald bearded guy took her place. He told the parents that if they wanted a "companion animal," they had to fill out an application form. I started talking with the oldest kid, and Pip started talking with the youngest kid and told her she liked her yellow mittens, and suddenly a lady with a little ring in her nostril came and invited their family to meet the dogs.

When the lady with the nostril ring said, "Right this way," I made a face at Pip and hopped right up. Pip hesitated, but then she hopped up too! We tagged along as though we were Kid #5 and Kid #6!

The family was so excited about getting a dog that they didn't notice us sneaking in behind them. And the lady with the nostril ring was so happy that someone was *adopting* a pet rather than dropping one off that she didn't either.

The family followed the signs for dogs and turned left. Pip and I followed the signs for cats and turned right.

Soon we were standing in front of cages and cages of cats! It was like a wall of cats!

Each cat had a food bowl, water bowl, litter box, and soft cloth. Some were asleep, but most were wide-awake. One poked his nose out, and another poked his paw out, and another twitched his ears. There was an old white cat and an old black cat pacing back and forth, back and forth. I wondered if they were senile felines (S-E-N-I-L-E-F-E-L-I-N-E-S), which is a palindrome I came up with recently. Then I felt bad for wondering that. Poor cats!

On the cages were clipboards with pieces of paper. They said things like "indoor cat" and "outdoor cat" and "finicky eater" and "not good with other cats." One said "gentle with children." Another said "may require time to warm up to new people."

"Where's the one that got hurt?" Pip asked. We both knew that we needed to find him before someone found us!

"I'm *looking*!!" I said. And I was! I was searching and searching for the honey-colored cat. I did not want to fall in love with the wrong cat by mistake!

Pip spotted a sign about "adoption options." It said that if you couldn't provide a "forever home," maybe you could provide a "foster home." She read it out loud and said, "Think we can talk Mom and Dad into letting us have a cat for a month?"

"I don't want a cat for a month!" I said. "I want a *forever* cat! And I want the one we came to find!"

But where was the cat with the bitten-up ear and soft white zigzag?

We walked down the hall and entered a second room filled with nothing but kittens. Observation: the only thing cuter than a wall of cats is a wall of kittens! The room smelled a little tiny bit of cat pee (kitten pee?) but I didn't even mind because the kittens were *seriously* cute—probably because they were so *unserious*. One was swatting a ball. Another yawned a big yawn, and then started closing its eyes and flopped over—fast asleep on its food bowl. Another was napping *inside* its litter box. Each cage had one toy and two or three (or even four!) kittens, and most were licking each other and playing and tumbling. One fluffy gray kitten stood on its hind legs and put out a front paw as if to high-five me. It was hard not to fall head-over-heels in love—but I resisted because I'd made up my mind about which cat I wanted to save.

Pip pointed out a sign that said: "Please adopt kittens in pairs." She looked at me and said, "I wish we could."

Just then a short lady with a long braid walked in. "Hello, girls." She was carrying a cage and must have assumed we were allowed to be there.

"Hello," we chimed and followed her back to the room with the grown-up cats.

The volunteer placed the cage on top of a row of other cages. "This yellow tabby arrived this morning," she said, adjusting the clipboard. "Got himself into quite a scuffle, poor fella."

Pip and I walked over to the yellow tabby. He looked at me with big, sad, round green eyes. He was like a skinny lion cub with a white Harry Potter zigzag above his nose. His right leg was also white, as if he'd broken it and was wearing a cat cast. And the tip of his tail was white, as if he'd dipped it into paint.

Pip and I both knew this was the cat we'd come to find! I looked at him and he looked at me, and I wished I could adopt him right then and there!

"He's a bit skittish," the lady said.

"Scottish?" Pip said.

"Skittish," the lady repeated. "Frightened. You know, a scaredy-cat. But who can blame him? He's been through a lot."

"How much does he cost?" I asked.

Pip stared at me, eyes wide.

"Kittens come with a small price tag—unless you take two," the lady answered. "But older cats are free. We *want* them to find good homes."

"Can I put this one on hold?" I asked.

"That's not our policy." She smiled. "But you may spend a few minutes with him to see if it would be a good fit. And your parents can fill out an application stating that they understand that pet ownership is a big commitment and responsibility." We did not mention that our parents were not with us and didn't even know we were there. "Cats can live fifteen to twenty years," the lady continued, "so we always check references. But if everything goes smoothly, you can take him home today. I bet he'd like that."

She gave the cat a smile, and the cat gave me a blink, and I wished I *could* promise him a forever home.

"Would you like me to go over this with your parents?" the lady asked. Pip and I exchanged a look and said, "No!" at the exact same time.

I wanted to say, "Jinx!" but instead mumbled, "Thanks anyway." Then Pip and I hurried off and raced downstairs and out of the building.

Outside, we started biking the three blocks to Taco Time. Pip was just ahead of me.

"He neeeeeeds us!" I called up to her.

"If we get to keep him," Pip shouted back, "we could name him van Gogh."

"Van Gogh?"

"Because of his ear!" she shouted. Pip has a poster of van Gogh sunflowers and once told me that when van Gogh couldn't sell any paintings, he got so upset and unstable that he cut off a piece of his ear and mailed it to a woman. Or something.

Well, I did not want to name our cat after a depressed artist with mismatched ears! So I said so—or shouted so.

"You have any better ideas?" Pip shouted back.

I considered saying, "Dandelion!" because then we could call him Dandy. But the cat's fur was more *lion*-colored than *dandelion*-colored. I also considered saying, "Honey," but he was a tough tomcat so that wouldn't work. I shouted, "Not yet."

Pip and I got to Taco Time and parked our bikes. I was trying and trying to come up with the perfect name, but I couldn't think of one. We ordered and our tacos arrived, and soon I was staring at mine and suddenly it occurred to me that the hurt cat was the exact same color as my…taco!

"I've got it!" I said a little too loudly. "Taco!" I couldn't believe what my brilliant brain came up with next. "No! Wait!" I said. "His name is… *Taco Cat!* T-A-C-O-C-A-T! It's a palindrome!"

"That's genius!" Pip said, and I could feel myself beaming. "But you'll never be able to convince B-O-B and A-N-N-A." To be funny, Pip spelled out our parents' names.

"Never say 'never,'" I said.

I will now stop writing because my hand is about to fall off. (Figuratively, not literally.)

AVA WREN, FUTURE CAT OWNER?

12/29
AFTER DINNER, WHICH WAS STEW

DEAR DIARY,

Pip's boyfriend texted Pip a photo of a big lungfish in the Shedd Aquarium. She texted him back a photo of the little catfish in our ABC book. Then Ben texted her a whole *school* of fish. From the face she made, you'd think he'd sent her a box of chocolates.

I just looked up "school of fish," and here are ten more good expressions:

1. A kindle of kittens
2. A prickle of hedgehogs
3. A troop of monkeys
4. A band of gorillas
5. A pride of lions
6. A leap of leopards
7. A tower of giraffes
8. A zeal of zebras
9. A flamboyance of flamingos
10. An exaltation of larks

A bunch of people is called a *crowd*, but there's no expression for a bunch of wrens—besides *flock*.

If I could invent one for my birthday, I'd invent "a wonder of wrens."

WONDERFUL AVA WREN WHO WANTS WONDERFUL TACO CAT

12/29
BEDTIME

DEAR DIARY,

Pip and I made a drum fish and an electric eel. The electric eel, I'm sorry to report, is pretty ugly.

Funny that some things are *pretty ugly*, but nothing is *ugly pretty*.

This is my eel poem:

E is for electric eel.

The electric eel looks like a worm or a snake.
Beware, beware of the shock it can make.

I wish I could *shock* my parents and tell them that we *are* adopting a cat, instead of having to ask (or beg).

AVA, ASKING ABOUT ADOPTING AN ANIMAL

12/30
RIGHT BEFORE DINNER

DEAR DIARY,

Pip and I didn't know whether to tell Mom and Dad that we went to the rescue center. We didn't want to lie, but we also didn't want to get in trouble if they found out.

Finally I decided to spill all to Dad. A few weeks ago, Mom and Dad both said I should speak my mind. Besides, my birthday is in two days, and parents don't ground kids right before their birthdays, do they?

While Dad was paying bills, I got out thirteen index cards and wrote one letter on each. When I finished, I made a fan out of them so Dad could see it was a palindrome: W-A-S-I-T-A-C-A-T-I-S-A-W.

"Was it a cat I saw?" Dad read. "Good one, Ava!"

"Dad, Pip and I *did* see a cat," I said. "We went looking for that injured cat Mom told us about. And we *found* him!"

"What do you mean 'found' him?"

"At the rescue center."

Dad looked more puzzled than mad. Maybe now that Pip is a teenager and not as shy as she used to be, he doesn't object to our doing some things on our own?

Weird that Pip is old enough to be independent and wear a bra and have a boyfriend!

I don't want to be independent or wear a bra or have a boyfriend. I just want Taco Cat!

I told Dad all about him, even his name.

"T-A-C-O-C-A-T? That's clever." Dad laughed. "But, Ava, you know Mom doesn't want a pet."

"I know." I wanted to add that it's not fair that Mom gets to spend all day with tons of animals when we don't even have one. "But I almost wish we had a mouse problem," I said. "Like, an *explosion* of mice."

And that's when I got an idea. An amazing idea. It was so amazing, I decided to call Maybelle and ask her to come over and help me with an "art project." (Dad said we could have a short after-dinner playdate since it's still vacation.)

But when I called Maybelle, she said, "Zara asked if she could sleep over, and I said okay and now we're about to have dinner. Can she come too?"

"I guess," I mumbled, surprised that Maybelle was having a sleepover with Zara, a girl who had just moved to Misty Oaks in September. Since when did my best-friend-since-first-grade have sleepovers with anyone besides *me*? To be honest, the thought of Maybelle and Zara having dinner together or even microwaving marshmallows made my stomach lurch.

Next I called my neighbors, Carmen and Lucia. I could hear Carmen asking her mom in Spanish if they could come over. Their parents are from Peru. Carmen and Lucia are twins and they each have a Paddington Bear. They say their bears are twins from Peru too.

I wish I could speak Spanish. I wish I were bilingual instead of just lingual. People say I have a "way with words," but I know only one language—so far.

I went into Pip's room. She was illustrating our F page:

F is for flying fish.

This lucky fast fish has wings and can fly.
When mean fish swim close, it jumps ten feet high.

"Pip," I asked, "do you know how to draw mice?"

She made a face and said, "Duh."

"Good," I said and told her my amazing idea—my amazing *plan*. She said it sounded dumb—but she got right to work.

AVA THE AMAZING

12/30
9:09 P.M.

Dear Diary,

Six people in one bedroom is pretty squooshy, but we sat in a circle: Pip and me, Carmen and Lucia, Maybelle and Zara. Pip showed us all her life-size drawing of a model house mouse. It had dot eyes, round ears, short whiskers, a curly tail, and (I don't know how Pip does this) kind of a cute personality. I gave everyone a pencil and scissors, and in the middle, we put a stack of paper, erasers, and a pencil sharpener.

"Why are we making paper mice?" Carmen asked. She and Lucia were both wearing green. They don't dress exactly the same, but they always wear the same color.

"Because my birthday is the day after tomorrow and I want a pet cat." I said that I wanted to show our parents how practical a cat could be.

"Practical?" Maybelle asked.

"Like, what if we had a *mouse invasion*?"

"I don't get it," Zara said. She crossed her legs, but not the crisscross applesauce way. She crossed them yoga style, feet on top. I wondered if she thought mouse-making was immature. Was it? "What are you going to do with all the mice?"

"Put them all over the furniture," I said. "First thing tomorrow, before our mom and dad wake up."

Zara looked like she didn't quite get it. (Confession: I didn't quite get what she was doing on my bedroom floor.) She shrugged and said, "I once had a pet guinea pig."

"In Peru, people *eat* guinea pigs," Carmen replied.

"Ewww!" Zara said.

"They roast them on spits," Lucia added.

"Did you ever try one?" Zara asked, squinching her face.

"They're yummy with garlic and lemon," Lucia admitted, looking sheepish. (Note: *sheepish* is a funny word. No one ever looks cattish or doggish or guinea-piggish.)

"What happened to your guinea pig?" Carmen asked.

"My cousin got to keep it when I had to move in with my grandparents," Zara answered, putting down her scissors.

It was strange having this new girl in my room. Were we supposed to ask about her family? Or *not* ask? After an awkward moment, Carmen said, "We once had pet mice."

"All they did was multiply!" Lucia added.

"It was disgusting!" Carmen said.

Pip wasn't saying much of anything. She was being as quiet as she used to be. Probably because of Zara.

I decided to tell the Aesop fable "The Country Mouse and the City Mouse." The twins like it when I tell fables, so I even spiced it up a little:

A country mouse invites a city mouse for dinner, but there's nothing to eat besides a little pile of beans. Then the city mouse, who is snobby, invites the country mouse to come dine with him. The two mice sneak into a fancy banquet hall and are about to dig into delicious leftovers—everything from lobster to banana splits. But no sooner do they start nibbling at what's left of the feast, than a hungry cat and giant barking dog chase them into a hole.

"That's it?" Zara asked.

"What's the moral?" Lucia asked.

"It's better to eat beans in peace than lobster in danger," I said.

"Or maybe it has to do with making new friends?" Zara said.

"I don't think so," I said because I didn't, and because I didn't like that Zara was making friends with *my* friends.

"You know what?" Maybelle said. "We're making *suburban* mice!"

"I just made three *blind* mice!" Carmen said. "Look!"

Lucia looked, then quickly erased the eye dots from three of her mice. "Me too!" she chimed, and they both started humming "Three Blind Mice."

Did Zara think the twins were being babyish?

Maybelle said, "Did you know that if you hold your nose, you can't hum?"

"Really?" Pip said.

"Really!" Maybelle said and told us all to start humming "Three Blind Mice." We did, even Zara. Maybelle raised her arms as if she were conducting a symphony. "On your marks, get set, go!" she said and held her nose, so we all held our noses. She was right: Our mouse-making factory fell silent! You can't hum and hold your nose at the same time!

After we'd made many, many mini mice (alliteration alert!),

Pip got out *Alphabet Fish*, and Zara started asking questions. I know asking questions is *consider*ed *considera*te, but she was asking a *lot* of questions. She asked why we were making a book (because we felt like it), and why it was about fish (because Pip likes fish), and if we'd ever made a book together before (no), and if Pip took art classes (yes), and if I took writing classes (no), and what G was going to be for (goldfish).

She said, "G could be for guppy."

I said Pip and I had already decided that G was going to be for goldfish.

Zara said, "Guppy sounds cuter." I looked at Maybelle to see if she thought Zara was being a bossy busybody, but Maybelle was admiring Pip's illustrations. "And I like the title *Something Fishy*," Zara added.

"The title is *Alphabet Fish*," I replied in a firm voice. Carmen and Lucia exchanged a worried look. "And G is for goldfish," I stated, "in honor of our pet goldfish who died." I almost told her that we'd named her Goldy Lox because LOX and LOCKS are homonyms: "lox," like smoked fish, and "locks," like the blond hair of the girl with the three bears, so it was a funny punny name. But I didn't want Zara to ask any more questions.

Soon Maybelle's mom came to pick up Maybelle and Zara so they could have their stupid sleepover. Maybelle's mom said she could drop the twins off too, "no problem."

But it *was* a problem because when everyone climbed into the same car, talking and laughing, I felt a twinge of loneliness. (Actually, a few twinges.)

By the time I went back upstairs, Pip was in bed with a book, and I knew she wouldn't want to talk. So I got in bed too and started writing in you.

I wish Taco Cat were here to keep me company.

Ava, Alone with a Mountain of Mice

12/30
MIDDLE OF THE NIGHT

DEAR DIARY,

I just turned on the light-up pen that Bea gave me, the one her parents sell at their bookshop. I wanted to double-check that my alarm was set for 6:45 a.m. so I could sneak down and do what I had to do.

I was also curious about how you say a "bunch of mice," so I looked it up. Guess what? It's a "*mischief* of mice"!

AVA THE MISCHIEVOUS

12/31
6:55 A.M.

Dear Diary,

I did it!

You know how in *Goodnight Moon*, there's a mouse peeking out on every single page? That's how it looks downstairs! There are mice everywhere! On chairs and on the sofa and bookshelf and floor and windowsill and coffee table...you name it, I put a mouse on it. I even put two in the fridge!

Now that it's (almost) daytime, a teeny tiny part of me wonders if this whole plan is dumb. Or if Mom will get mad.

Oh well, too late!

As Dad says when he's quoting Shakespeare, "What's done, is done."

In fifteen minutes, Dad and Mom will wake up and see my mischief of mice. (My *mess* of mice?) I put one on Dad's desk with a note that says, "All I want for my birthday is T-A-C-O-C-A-T. I will take excellent care of him. Pleeeeeeeeeeeeeeeeease."

The "please" might have even more e's. I didn't count.

I keep thinking about Taco Cat. I hope we can get him and that no one else adopts him first. I'm not too worried because

Mom says kittens are more popular than cats, especially "cats with issues." (According to Mom, mismatched ears are an "issue," even though mismatched eyes are considered a good thing, spelled *heterochromia*.)

Poor Taco! He probably feels so lost and alone!

I remember once when I felt lost and alone.

I was about three, and Mom and I had gone shopping in a giant department store. I don't know if Mom got distracted or if I did, but suddenly the high heel shoes next to me did *not* look familiar. I looked up, and the lady next to me was *not* my mother! I burst into tears. Where was my mom? Would I ever see her again??

The lady with the high heel shoes took me to a security guard and next thing you know, a loudspeaker announcement said: "Will the woman who lost her daughter please report to the information desk?" I stood there with a bunch of strangers for what felt like a really long time until finally Mom came *clip clip clipping* over. I guess the security people could tell by my expression that she was not a kidnapper, and Mom swooped me up and took me home.

I wish I could swoop Taco Cat up and take him home.

I'm really tired, but I'm trying to stay awake until it gets light outside. It's already officially New Year's Eve, which means it's almost New Year's Day—and my eleventh birthday! A new year and new age!

I'm practically falling asleep though. If I were a cat, I would have conked out in my food bowl.

Maybe I'll go back to sleep for just five more minutes and get up when Mom and Dad get up.

Ava in Anticipation

12/31
New Year's Eve Morn

Dear Diary,

I slept until 10:30! I did not mean to do that! I meant to wake up hours ago so I could see Mom and Dad's reaction!

Not only did I oversleep, but just now, I banged my funny bone. It was not one bit *funny*!

Mom must already be at work. She says vets work all the time because animals get sick all the time. Dr. Gross works every day except Sunday, and even on Sunday, someone has to go to the clinic to feed and check on all the animals.

Question: Did Mom and Dad like my mice?

Bigger question: Will they let me have a cat??

Time to find out!

Ava, Awake

12/31
11:11

Dear Diary,

I opened my door and saw a trail of mice. It went all the way from my room to Dad's desk! One little mousie after another! I figured this *had* to be a good sign.

"Did you find them all?" I asked Dad.

"Good morning, Sleepy Head," he said. "Yes, I think we did."

"Even the pair in the cheese drawer?"

"You put mice inside the fridge?"

"Just two," I said *sheepishly* (but not mouseishly). "What did Mom think?"

"Actually, she thought it was funny. She knows this means a lot to you."

"Really?"

"Really. You did a good job of expressing yourself."

I said thanks, and Dad told me a story about when he and Mom were housesitting when they were newlyweds. They bought a little bag of fancy chocolate-covered almonds and left them on the kitchen counter. In the middle of the night, they heard a loud clattering and were afraid burglars had broken in. So they went downstairs and turned on the lights. No one was there, but the bag of chocolates was empty, and on the kitchen floor, they saw itty-bitty mouse droppings! The cat burglars were…a *mischief of mice*!

I laughed and planned to tell that story to Chuck in school. He is pretty much the only fifth-grade boy I talk to, and we like to make each other laugh. I've known him even longer than I've known Maybelle, because in kindergarten we sat next to each other on the bus on an apple-picking field trip.

"So can I get Taco Cat for my birthday?" I asked Dad straight out.

Dad pushed back his big brown chair and did not say no. He said, "Want to run some errands? You and Pip went through a lot of paper last night."

I said, "Sorry," even though I could tell Dad wasn't mad. He likes it when Pip and I do "creative projects" together.

"What do you think: Great Wall or Taco Time?" Dad asked.

"Taco Time! Should I wake up Pip?"

"At your own risk," Dad said because lately Pip has been waking up grumpy. I took the stairs two at a time, and with each giant step, I could feel myself coming up with a brand-new plan.

"Pip!" I said, knocking and barging in at the same time. "Get up!" I started talking a mile a minute.

Pip opened her eyes and listened. "It'll never work," she said, sounding like the big brother in *The Carrot Seed*. The one who doesn't believe in his little brother's little seed and says, "It won't come up."

"You should be more optimistic," I said.

"You should be less annoying," she said.

But here's the thing: she's getting dressed, so I think she *is* willing to give my plan a try.

Ava, Full of Plans

12/31
1:30 P.M.
AT THE RESCUE CENTER!

DEAR DIARY,

At Taco Time, Dad asked if I knew how to spell "quesadilla" and "guacamole." I spelled both words, no peeking and *no problema*. So far in fifth grade, I've gotten nothing but 100s on all my spelling tests. English is by far my best subject. (I stink at math, which is Maybelle's best subject, and I'm only okay at gym, which is Chuck's best subject.)

After lunch, Pip told Dad that we wanted to take him "on a field trip." Dad looked suspicious, and I stayed quiet (M-U-M). Pip was saying everything exactly as we'd planned. "The rescue center is really nearby," she casually remarked.

"The rescue center?" Dad made a face, then said, "Oh, why not?"

Pip gave me a little kick under the table, so I gave her a little kick back. We both know that deep down, Dad is a mushball when it comes to us kids. And deep down, maybe he likes cats as much as we do.

While we were walking the three blocks, Dad started rambling about how writers and cats are natural companions. He said that James Joyce wrote about cats, and so did Charles Dickens and

Mark Twain. He said Ernest Hemingway left money in his will for his cats in Key West, Florida, "and some were polydactyl."

"Polywhat?" I said.

"Polydactyl. It means having extra toes." Dad said that most cats have five toes on their front feet and four on their back, but "mitten kittens" are born with extras.

"H-U-H," I said, because our family likes spelling out palindromes. I was trying to picture "mitten kittens" and trying to picture myself as a famous writer known for her children's books and her faithful furry feline friend, Taco.

"T. S. Eliot," Dad added, "wrote cat poems that got turned into the Broadway musical."

"*Cats*," Pip said.

I thought about T. S. Eliot and said, "If you take the S away, his name backward is T O I L E T."

Dad laughed. Pip said, "Dad, it's mostly your fault we're word nerds!" (which is true, even though Mom must have agreed to name us P-I-P H-A-N-N-A-H and A-V-A E-L-L-E).

Anyway, we're now at the rescue center. Ponytail Lady said that before we could go upstairs, Dad had to fill out a form. So when Dad started writing, I did too.

Gotta go! Here comes Nostril Ring Lady!

Ava, About to See Animals

12/31
AN HOUR LATER

DEAR DIARY,

Nostril Ring Lady escorted us upstairs, past the barking dogs, and into the cat rooms. Then the short lady with the long braid came in and said, "I remember you girls!" I asked if our cat was still there, and she winked and said, "He's been asking about you." She was carrying a cage with a *kindle* of kittens.

Dad and Pip and I stayed in the room with the older cats, and at first, I didn't see Taco anywhere. I looked and looked, but...no Taco. What if she was wrong? What if someone *had* adopted my yellow tabby? We kept searching and searching.

Suddenly I noticed a cage on the floor in the corner. And there he was! I saw his green eyes and taco-colored fur and jagged ear and white leg and little zigzag. He was looking right at me! It was like he was *waiting*—just *waiting*—for me to recognize him. Our eyes met and my heart melted!

I sat on the floor, put my face near his cage, reached in, and tried to pet him with my fingertips. He seemed nervous and was still skinny, but not as skinny as when I first saw him.

"Dad," I said. "I found him! He neeeeeeds us." I reminded

Dad for the quintillionth time that Taco was all I wanted for my birthday—and that my birthday was *tomorrow*.

Pip said, "Dad, let's just do it. Let's get him!"

"We have to talk to Mom," Dad said, which meant he was at least considering it. Then he looked into Taco's big sad eyes and whispered, "Buddy, this might be your lucky day."

Ava, Full of Hope

12/31
4:25 P.M.
IN OUR CAR

DEAR DIARY,

Believe it or not, we are in the car outside Dr. Gross's clinic waiting for Mom! She's getting off early because it's New Year's Eve. When she walks out, Dad and Pip and I are going to surprise her and drive her straight to the rescue center!

In my almost eleven years in Misty Oaks, I'd never once been to the rescue center, but this will be my *second* time today and my *third* time this week!

Dad said not to get our hopes up, but of course our hopes are up. Mine are sky-high! They are as high as Mount Everest, which Maybelle once said is over 29,000 feet high and the highest mountain in the world.

While we sat in the car, Dad told us that Mom is the only person in Dr. Gross's practice who doesn't have a pet. I knew that Dr. Gross has a dog named Cowboy, and the front desk lady and her partner have three cats (one has just one eye), and one of the technicians has a ferret, and another has a canary, but I did not know that *everybody* has a pet except Mom.

Right now, Pip and I are in the backseat, and while I'm writing, Pip is illustrating my H poem:

H is for hammerhead shark.

The great hammerhead shark is a scary beast.
If it saw you at sea, it would think: What a feast!

It is almost 4:30 p.m.

In seven and a half hours, at midnight, I will be eleven.

In one hour, will I have a cat?

Gotta go! Here comes Mom!!

Ava with Fingers Crossed

New Year's Eve Night

Dear Diary,

Mom said yes!!!

I have a cat!!!

His name is Taco!!!

❤❤❤❤

Ava

1/1
MY BIRTH~~DAY~~ NIGHT

DEAR DIARY,

Last night, I woke up and it was pitch-black outside. I wasn't sure if the glittery Times Square ball had or hadn't dropped, or if it was or wasn't my birthday. Was it a new year? Was I a new age: 11 on 1/1?

All I knew for sure was that Taco was 100 percent *mine*!

I have a pet cat!!!

We brought him home in a cat carrier, but Mom said we had to keep him in the bathroom the first night. That didn't seem very welcoming, but Mom said that when a cat is not "accustomed to a new environment," it's best to take things slowly, and that Taco would feel safest in a "small, confined space." I was so glad we'd actually adopted him—and bought canned food and pet bowls and kitty litter—that I didn't object.

Right before I went upstairs, I told Taco that he was the best birthday present in the whole wide world. He still seemed scared (skittish?), so I didn't pick him up, but I petted him and told him I'd be back first thing in the morning.

Well, this morning, he was curled up on the bathmat. He'd

eaten some food and used his litter box and even covered his P-O-O-P with sand, which cats do. Mom said these were all "good signs." She showed me how to scoop out his dried doodies and shake off the sand and flush the P-O-O-P down the toilet. I told Pip it reminded me of the game we used to play by Nana Ethel's creek called "Panning for Gold." Pip said I was crazy, but I knew she remembered Panning for Gold as well as I did. (I like that we have a lot of the same memories.)

Anyway, Mom and Dad had said they'd take me and my friends out for pizza for my birthday, but I didn't want to leave Taco alone that long. So I called Maybelle and Bea and Carmen and Lucia and invited them to come here instead.

Bea and Ben had just gotten back from vacation, and she said she'd be right over. She's two years older than me, but we became friends last fall. That's when she and I came up with the five Pip Pointers to help Pip shake off her shyness.

Well, everyone got to meet my new cat—but not in the way I was hoping.

I'd pictured Taco taking turns climbing onto their laps, purring and kneading. Kneading is what cats do when they press their little paws against you one at a time, left and right, right and left. Mom said that newborn kittens knead and purr when they nurse because that's how they tell their mother to stay still. Grown cats knead and purr mostly when they are relaxed and happy.

Taco did not knead or purr at all.

What happened was this: We all stood by the bathroom door. Bea and Pip were on tiptoe, Maybelle and I were in the middle, and the twins were crouching down (dressed in matching yellow). The plan was for me to open the door a crack so everyone could peek at Taco, asleep on the bathmat. I did—but Taco dashed out! He made a beeline (cat line?) for the sofa! And he's been hiding underneath it ever since!

All anyone saw was a flash of fur!

Before I could stop them, Carmen and Lucia raced after him and got on their stomachs and started groping under the sofa. Not only did Taco *not* come out, he *hissed* at them! He even grumble-growled! It was a strange, low, unhappy sound.

Mom said we needed to let him get comfortable on his own terms. She also said that adult cats don't meow to other cats, they meow only to people, usually to "ask for food or water or space."

Well, we let Taco have some space while I opened birthday presents. Maybelle gave me a rainbow-colored beaded bracelet that she'd made just for me. The twins gave me a gold picture frame (which I like) and a fuzzy pink jewelry box (which I don't). Bea gave me a book of funny cat photographs from her parents' shop. Pip gave me a scarf. And everyone sang, "Happy Birthday!" and ate pizza and cake.

Now that I'm eleven, I wonder if I seem a lot older than the twins, who are in fourth grade. I also wonder if I seem a lot younger than Bea and Pip, who are in seventh. Am I growing up at the right speed?

I can hardly believe I'm eleven. I won't be a palindrome age again until I'm twenty-two!

Ava Wren, Birthday Girl

1/2 (WHICH LOOKS LIKE ONE-HALF BUT MEANS JANUARY 2) SATURDAY 11:30 A.M.

DEAR DIARY,

This morning Pip and I were playing Battleship. I was trying to locate her submarine and said, "B-7?"

She said, "BELIEVE."

I said, "BEWARE!"

She said, "BEHOLD!"

I said, "BEHAVE!"

She said, "BEEHIVE!"

We both laughed, and she said, "Ava, come with me to Bates Books."

I said I wanted to stay with Taco. But Pip pleaded—and even offered me a pack of bubblemint gum. I knew she was hoping to run into Ben since Bea and Ben's parents own the bookstore and Pip hadn't seen him since vacation started. Finally I said okay—if we made it quick.

We bundled up and off we went, but Ben wasn't there and neither was Bea. Their fluffy orange and white cat, Meow Meow, was, and he rubbed against us, his tail high in the air. He is as sweet as a…Creamsicle!

Guess who else was there? Chuck! He looked different because he'd gotten a haircut and maybe gotten a little taller since last week? (Is that possible?) He also had a Band-Aid under his chin—the tan kind, not the cartoon character kind.

Mrs. Bates was helping him find a book about a boxer. She's good at helping kids pick out books. When Chuck saw me, he came over, so Mrs. Bates started helping Pip instead. She was telling her about some "new YA paperbacks." YA stands for young adult. (Confession: I don't think of Pip as a Young Adult. I think of her as a Big Kid.)

Well, I told Chuck about our new cat, and he told me a joke:

Question: Why did ten cats jump off a bridge?

Answer: They were copycats.

He expected me to laugh, but I said, "That's not funny. That's sad." I was picturing a soggy bunch of forlorn felines.

He said, "Ava, it's a *joke*, and besides, cats have nine lives!"

I rolled my eyes, and he asked what I was going to buy. I said, "A pen," and he helped me pick out a striped pen covered in orange and black velvety cloth with a tiger's head.

"What's a cat's favorite color?" he asked.

"What?"

"Purrrrple!"

This time I did laugh, and I also poked him in the ribs and he poked me back. I asked what happened to his chin (he tripped), and then he said he had to go because his mom was waiting for him.

Pip was still "browsing," so I found a coffee table book about cats in paintings and took it to an alcove with giant pillows. The origami snowflakes I'd made for Mrs. Bates last month were still on the walls. Meow Meow came and stretched out by my feet, and even though I wanted to check on Taco Cat, I felt happy with Meow Meow, waiting for Pip and looking at colorful cats.

I've liked Bates Books since I was little, even before Bea and Ben switched into our middle school.

It's true that I like short books, not long books, and that I am not an "avid reader" like Pip. But I really like bookstores—especially cozy ones with fluffy cats.

If I ever had to be stuck—stranded!—overnight somewhere and I could pick where, I would definitely pick a cozy bookstore.

I could see how a kid might *think* she'd want to spend the night in a candy store, but that would get boring and you'd end up with a stomachache. A rescue center might sound fun, but that would get noisy and you'd feel sorry for the animals. And a zoo or an amusement park would definitely get creepy at night.

But a bookshop, if you kept all the lights on, could be nice.

And you wouldn't get bored. Even if you were locked in for *hours*! Plus, if you got lonely at night, you could read *Goodnight Moon* or *Owl Moon* or *Many Moons* or *Kitten's First Full Moon* or any bedtime book, even one without a moon or a cat. And if you got tired of reading, you could look at pop-up books and coffee table books.

I started thinking about words on screens versus words in books. Like, with texting or Facebook, you can read what people are thinking *right that very second*. But with books, you can read what people took *ages* to think about. Some authors take years and years to write a book that a reader can gobble up in hours, which, for the reader, is a very good deal.

Paintings are like that too. An artist works on them for a long time, but you can enjoy them in a short time.

Anyway, even though I was enjoying looking at cat paintings with Meow Meow, after a while I wanted to check on my own cat, so I showed Pip my favorite pages then said, "Let's go."

Pip said okay, and she bought two books and I bought my pen and we went home.

Guess what? We hadn't missed a thing because Taco hadn't come out from under the sofa!

He still hasn't!

Dad said we need to be patient. Mom said you can't rush a cat.

Since Dad had told Pip and me about writers and cats, I told Dad and Mom about artists and cats, and the book I'd been looking at. I said that Goya painted spooky cats, and Picasso painted pointy cats, and Renoir and Cassatt painted soft, cuddly cats. I also said, "If Pip drew Taco, it would be a drawing of a sofa." Everybody laughed.

Ava, Amusing

1/2
Saturday Night

Dear Diary,

Maybelle invited me over after lunch, but I was positive Taco was going to come out and I didn't want to miss the big moment, so I said I couldn't. What I didn't know was that Taco was planning to spend the *whole entire afternoon* under the sofa!

At night, when we're asleep, he creeps out and eats and uses the litter box. But during the day, all he does is hide. I've been getting on the floor and lifting the flap of the sofa to check on him. It's like lifting a curtain, except there's no show.

At least he doesn't hiss or grumble or growl. He just stares. And sometimes backs away.

I want Taco to be happy, but I wish he'd hurry up about it!

Ava, Impatient

1/3 (WHICH LOOKS LIKE ONE-THIRD BUT MEANS JANUARY 3)
SUNDAY MORNING, STILL IN BED

DEAR DIARY,

Next to my bed, along with my diary, I always have *Aesop's Fables*, and I just dog-eared the cat fables.

Isn't that funny: *dog*-eared the *cat* fables?

I also reread "Belling the Cat." Here's how it goes:

A bunch of scared mice come out of their holes to have an emergency meeting. They are trying to decide what to do about a hungry cat that won't stop sneaking up on them. Finally a young mouse says he has solved the problem. "We should put a bell on the cat," he states, "so we can hear it coming." The mice all think this is a great idea—until a wise senior citizen mouse says, "And which of you would like to put the bell on the cat?"

The moral: "It's easy-peasy to *have* a great idea, but that's just the beginning."

My great idea was to adopt a grown-up, scratched-up, funny-looking cat.

What if it wasn't a great idea? What if it was a horrible idea?

AVA, AGGRAVATED AESOP ADMIRER

1/3
Sunday Evening

Dear Diary,

Maybelle called this morning to invite me to go with her family to the circus and dinner in the city. I knew that would take all day so I said I'd better stay home because Taco was bound to come out.

Maybelle said, "Really? You sure?" She sounded disappointed.

When I hung up, I peeked under the sofa, and Taco wasn't even there! I looked all around the living room and downstairs, and he was nowhere to be seen. I searched upstairs and finally found him under Mom and Dad's bed. I told Mom and Dad everything, and they said to call Maybelle right back and tell her I changed my mind.

I did, but it was too late! Maybelle said she was sorry, but her parents had bought an extra ticket and wanted her to invite someone, and then Zara called, so she invited her.

"It's okay," I said, even though of course it wasn't. When we hung up, my throat was so tight, I could barely swallow. Why hadn't I said yes to Maybelle?

Pip could tell I was upset and suggested we work on *Alphabet*

Fish. She said her art teacher, Ms. Richichi, says doing something creative always helps you feel better.

Well, Pip and I worked on two pages, and it helped a little, but only a little. I think Pip might be more into this fish book than I am. Still, I did "I is for icefish" and:

J is for jellyfish.

The jellyfish looks like a clear parachute.
Do you think it's ugly or do you think it's cute?

Taco, by the way, is not ugly or cute. He is…invisible.

Confession: I'm actually glad school starts up again tomorrow even though that will mean waking up early and having homework. I miss seeing Maybelle and Chuck. And I like English—though I'm not sure how I'll feel about it now that Zara and Maybelle have started hanging out. (Did I used to think that *Zara* was invisible?)

I am about to go to sleep. I wish Taco were next to me, purring.

But he's not. I don't know where he is. I'm alone and trying not to be furious at myself for being too dumb to go to the circus. Am *I* a clown??

Sometimes at night, it's hard not to think bad thoughts. Like: What's wrong with me that all I wanted for my birthday was an injured old scaredy-cat? And what's wrong with Taco? Is he a D-U-D?

Grrrrrrrrr.

While we were brushing our teeth, Pip reminded me that our next page is "K is for kissing gourami." As a joke, I asked if she'd ever kissed Ben. She spat into the basin and said, "No!" Then she quietly added, "Not yet anyway."

I have to say, I am shocked. I can't picture Pip kissing anyone.

Then again, last year I could hardly picture Pip *talking* to anyone!

Ava, Astonished

1/4 (WHICH LOOKS LIKE ONE-QUARTER BUT—OH NEVER MIND!) 2:30

DEAR DIARY,

First day back in school! I'm in the library, by the big window.

Homeroom was fun. People were talking about their vacations, and even though ours was a "staycation," I got to tell everyone about Taco Cat.

Lunch was *not* fun. Maybelle sat next to me wearing a string necklace with a M on it, then Zara sat down wearing a string necklace with a Z on it!

At first, I thought they'd each gotten it for Christmas. Then I wondered: what if it *wasn't* a coincidence? Had Zara copied Maybelle? Was she a copy*cat*?

Just to be nice, I said, "I like your necklaces."

Zara said, "We got them yesterday! We got matching bracelets too." She put her hand out and dangled her bracelet. Maybelle put her hand out and dangled *her* bracelet. I wished I were at least wearing the rainbow bracelet Maybelle had beaded for my birthday, but I wasn't, so I kept my hands down.

They high-fived each other with their dumb dangly bracelets, and I felt like Taco: I wanted to run away and hide.

Worse, they were talking about the circus—the ringmaster and tightrope walkers and miniature ponies and jugglers and acrobats. They said two kids from the audience got to help a clown spin some plates.

"We loved that!" Zara said.

Well, I did *not* love the way Zara was saying "we" about Maybelle and her. Maybelle and I are supposed to be the "we"!

For once, I was glad that lunch period was ridiculously short. I don't think I could have sat there one more minute fake-liking their matching stuff and hearing about the oh-so-fun circus I'd stupidly missed.

When it was time for English, Maybelle and I sat down and Zara sat right next to us.

Mrs. Lemons began a unit about haiku. Haiku are poems that started in ancient Japan. They're pronounced "hi coo" and are made of three lines: five syllables, seven syllables, five syllables. Mrs. Lemons said they're often about the natural world—"seasons, plants, and animals"—and the best ones use imagery and "give readers something extra" to think about.

She gave us an example of a haiku that a poet named Basho wrote way back in the 1600s:

OBSERVED BY DAYLIGHT,

THE FIREFLY IS ONLY

A SIMPLE INSECT.

Then she asked us to write one in class and one for homework.

Since Mrs. Lemons once taught us that onomatopoeias are words that are spelled the way they sound, I tried to be extra creative. I wrote:

THE CRIES OF CATS ARE

ONOMATOPOETIC:

HISS, GROWL, MEOW, PURR.

We went around the room reading our haiku aloud. Maybelle's was about constellations, Chuck's was about icicles, and Riley's was about her pony (of course). Well, since you are my diary, I hope it doesn't count as boasting if I tell you that Mrs. Lemons *loved* my haiku. I swear, she wanted to marry it! (L-O-L)

Chuck liked it too and said, "I bet Ava even spelled 'onomatowhatever' right!" Everyone laughed.

Except me. I just smiled.

AVA, WHO WRITES HAIKU

P.S. Writing haiku is more fun than writing fish rhymes.
P.P.S. Writing in you is also more fun because a diary is like a really good friend who is always there and always listens and never goes off with anybody else.

1/4
BEDTIME

DEAR DIARY,

Taco Cat came out in the open today!

At least that's what Dad said. When Pip and I came home, Taco was back under the sofa, and all we could see was the tippy tip of his tail. Pip tried to lure him out with a phone charger cord, but he wouldn't come. I tried to coax him with yarn, and he started reaching for it with his front paws, but the phone rang and he went back under again. (It wasn't even a real phone call! It was a telemarketer!!)

After a gross "Meatless Monday" starring sweet potatoes and tofu (which Pip and I used to call Toe Food), I kneeled down by the sofa and lifted the flap. I was remembering how Bea and I had helped Pip come out of her shell with our Pip Pointers. They included making eye contact, saying hi, paying compliments, and asking questions. So I looked right at Taco Cat, said hi, told him how handsome he was, and asked about his stitched-up ear.

Taco did not say hi back, but he did blink at me. Twice. And I think he appreciated my attempt at human-feline communication.

Still, his behavior is frustrating! It makes *me* want to growl.

Mom said she is going to bring home some cat treats and that might help.

I thought about this for a while then announced that we could set up a reward drawer (R-E-W-A-R-D-D-R-A-W-E-R). I said we could put treats in there for us too, like licorice for her, M&M minis for Pip, and bubblemint gum for me.

Mom said the drawer should be just for Taco, but that maybe she'd bring home a cat brush too.

Anyway, after being excited about getting Taco, then disappointed by how much he hides, I am hopeful again. Dad says I'm keeping the faith.

Is keeping the faith like believing in happy endings?

A lot of kids' books have happy endings, but Aesop's fables mostly have morals.

Tonight, I got in my pajamas and tried to write the homework haiku. For a long time, I just looked out at the full moon, hoping for inspiration. Finally, I saw the old moon in a new way, so I started counting syllables on my fingers and wrote:

The full moon tonight

is caught in high branches, but

it will find its way.

Ava Wren, Patient Poet

1/5
BEFORE SCHOOL

Dear Diary,

All of us were having breakfast (except Taco), and Dad said, “One of the best things about being a grown-up is morning coffee.”

For some reason, I counted that out, and I said, “Hey! That’s a haiku!”

Mom said, “A haiku?”

“It’s 5-7-5!” I repeated the sentence aloud: “One of the best things / about be-ing a grown-up / is morn-ing cof-fee.”

Dad smiled but said that even though it was the right number of syllables, I couldn’t call it a “real haiku” any more than someone can read a phone book onstage and call it a play. “There’s math, and then there’s poetry.”

I said, “Number one, *phone books* are only in old movies. And number two, I know about real haiku.” I told him Basho had written over a thousand of them.

Pip said her Spanish teacher told her a Spanish palindrome: *Anita lava la tina* (A-N-I-T-A-L-A-V-A-L-A-T-I-N-A). It means: Anita washes the tub.

I said, "W-O-W."

Mom said we'd all better hurry up or we'd be late to school.

Ava Wren, Haiku Expert

1/5
AFTER SCHOOL

DEAR DIARY,

In school, we read our haiku aloud, and Mrs. Lemons said, "Ava, that is a real haiku!"

I felt proud—until I noticed Zara whispering to Maybelle. They were wearing their stupid matching bracelets.

Is Zara trying to take Maybelle away from me? Is she succeeding??

At the end of class, I decided to talk to Maybelle. But Mrs. Lemons said she wanted to talk to *me*, so I had to stay behind while Maybelle and Zara walked out together.

Mrs. Lemons asked if I thought Pip might want to make a poster of my moon haiku to hang in the hallway. She knows Pip is artistic because Pip used to be in her class.

I said I'd ask then tried to catch up to Maybelle and Zara. But I didn't see them anywhere! It made me feel all alone even though there were kids everywhere. It just hurts when your old friend makes new friends.

Back home, Pip said sure to illustrating my moon-in-a-tree haiku, so she got out thick poster paper and we started working quietly at the kitchen table.

Guess who came creeping over? Taco Cat!

I thought he was finally going to say a proper hello! And I liked his timing because I needed a cat cuddle. But all he did was sniff my sneakers—then dart inside an empty grocery bag.

Did he come out of his shell only to disappear into a bag??

Doesn't Taco know by now that I'd never try to hurt him? And why is everyone, from my cat to my BFF, running away from me?

Well, Taco didn't stay in the bag long, and when he emerged, I said, "Cat's out of the bag!" which was funny if I do say so myself. Pip half-smiled, but I could tell she was deep in the world of her drawing. That happens to me sometimes too: I start writing and lose track of everything else.

AVA, AUTHOR, NOT ARTIST

1/5
AN HOUR LATER

I wrote another haiku:

JANUARY SNOW

FLAKES FLOATING FLYING FALLING

WHISPERING WINTER

AVA, ALLITERATING

1/5
BEDTIME

Dear Diary,

Pip wanted to work on *Alphabet Fish*, but lunch was fish sticks and dinner was mahimahi (weird word), so I said I'd had enough fish for one day.

She said, "Oh, c'mon!"

I said, "You're my sister, not my boss!" She looked a little mad and a little sad, and that made me feel a little bad (especially since she had illustrated my moon haiku), so I scribbled a quick K rhyme:

K is for kissing gourami.

The kissing gourami do just as they please.
They kiss all day and don't care who sees.

When I handed it to Pip, she didn't say anything, but I swear, she blushed a little.

After dinner, I was struggling with my math homework and getting very distracted by Taco. He'd found a fly in the living room and was chasing it all around. It was as if he'd completely forgotten Dad and I were there. Dad and I gave each other a smile because Taco was finally making himself at home. But then Taco caught the fly with both paws, and we exchanged a frown because, well, it was disgusting that Taco ate a fly up as if it were a Raisinet!

Oh, that reminds me: Dad told me a math joke.

Question: What did the math teacher say when he was offered cake?

Answer: "I prefer pi."

Get it? I-P-R-E-F-E-R-P-I.

(H-O-H-O-H-O-H)

Pi, according to Maybelle, is a special specific number that starts with 3.1415 and never stops. Maybelle's family actually celebrates Pi Day each March 14. They make pie!

Anyway, I told Dad a math joke too.

Question: Why should you never argue with a ninety-degree angle?

Answer: Because it's always right.

Maybelle was the one who told me that joke.

Is she telling jokes to Zara now?

Sometimes I wish I had a remote control for my brain so I could change the channel and not think about things I don't want to think about. Is that one reason Pip likes books so much? Because she can just enter another universe and stay there as long as she wants?

AVA, WHO LIKES PIE MORE THAN PI (AND SOMETIMES WANTS TO CRY)

1/6
BEDTIME

DEAR DIARY,

Taco let me pet him! I was on the sofa, and he came and sat on the armrest under the lamp. I started petting him gently, and he didn't make a run for it. He stayed there—for at least thirty seconds.

I was so happy, *I* felt like purring!

Taco still hasn't purred, but Mom said he is "learning to trust us."

At dinner, which was drumsticks, Dad said that today Taco jumped onto his desk, stepped on his keyboard, and typed some pretend words.

I said, "Maybe Taco wants to be a writer too!"

Pip said, "He could go by T. C. Wren. And his books could be shelved next to E. B. White's."

I said, "I wonder what the E in E. B. White stands for."

Dad said, "Elwyn."

Pip and I looked at each other, stupefied (which is a bonus spelling word that means shocked, not stupid). We said, "Elwyn?!" and then, "Jinx!" and then spent the rest of dinner trying to think of other kids' book authors who use the initials of their first names. I came up with J. K. Rowling. Mom and Dad and Pip came up with:

- J. M. Barrie, who wrote *Peter Pan*
- A. A. Milne, who wrote *Winnie-the-Pooh*
- J. R. R. Tolkien, who wrote *The Hobbit*
- P. L. Travers, who wrote *Mary Poppins*
- C. S. Lewis, who wrote *The Lion, the Witch, and the Wardrobe*
- E. L. Konigsburg, who wrote *From the Mixed-Up Files of Mrs. Basil E. Frankweiler*
- S. E. Hinton, who wrote *The Outsiders*

Believe it or not, Pip has read all those books!

When authors use initials instead of names, readers don't know if a woman or a man wrote the book. But that shouldn't matter anyway, as long as the book is good.

I wonder if I really will be able to write kids' books someday. I hope so!

A. E. WREN

P.S. Here are the first names, in order, of all those authors: Joanne, James, Alan, John, Pamela, Clive, Elaine, and Susan. (No offense to E. B. White, but Elwyn is the weirdest name in the bunch.)

P.P.S. Zara is a weird name too.

1/7
AFTER SCHOOL

Dear Diary,

Today was a bad day.

At lunch, I sat with Maybelle, and naturally Zara came rushing over with her red tray and grilled cheese. Maybelle asked about Taco, and Zara said, "I thought its name was Paco." (She said "it" not "he," and "Paco" not "Taco.") "*His* name is *Taco Cat*," I said and explained that palindromes, like T-A-C-O-C-A-T, are spelled the same backward and forward. I also said that I'd gotten to pet him for almost a minute. Well, I could feel Zara looking at me as if I had a gnat on my nose, and I realized how lame that sounded—like my cat is an antisocial loser. And I'd even exaggerated!

Finally I decided to just go ahead and admit that it's hard because I'd wanted a cat and now that I have one, it's not like we hang out.

Zara said, "In my old school, I'd wanted a boyfriend, and when I got one, we didn't hang out either."

Maybelle laughed, but I didn't see what that had to do with *anything*.

Sometimes Zara says zany things. Maybe that was her way of

saying boys notice her. Which they do. Because she's new. And prettyish. And a little flirty.

When boys talk to her, she sometimes lights up and laughs. They sometimes do too! (Even Chuck!)

I don't understand flirting. How to do it or why you'd want to.

Question: Am I a *tom*boy with a *tom*cat?

"Your mom's a vet, right?" Zara asked.

"She manages the practice of a vet named Dr. Gross," I answered. "She does bookkeeping and deals with clients." Zara didn't say anything, and it was strange, feeling as if I had to defend my mom. "Sometimes she comes home with sad stories," I said and started babbling. "Like, about dogs who eat rocks or socks. Or lunatic bunnies who don't like being cooped up. Last month, a lady dropped her dog off for a shot and she didn't come back to pick him up! She *abandoned* him!"

I expected Zara to ask what happened because that's what people do when I tell pet stories. But Zara said, "Oh, so she's not actually a vet."

That bugged me, and when Zara switched from pets back to boys, things got worse. She said Pip and Ben make a "cute couple" and asked if they'd kissed. Pip hadn't liked when *I'd* asked that, and I knew she'd *hate* that other people were talking about them.

Zara even asked who I like. I said I didn't have a crush (because I don't) but added that I have friends who are guys (because I do). To give an example, I added, "Like Chuck." I might have smiled a tiny bit because I was remembering three dumb jokes he'd recently told me:

Question: How do you make a hot dog stand?

Answer: Take away his chair

Question: What's brown and sticky?

Answer: A stick.

Question: What did the dog on the roof say?

Answer: "Roof!"

Well, Zara said, "I can find out if he likes you."

"Of course he likes me," I said. Then I added, "But not *that* way!" Suddenly Zara was standing up, and I realized that she was going to talk to Chuck—and ruin everything! "Wait, no, no, don't *ask* him!" I blurted. "He and I are friends, just friends, and that's all we want to be!"

I looked at Maybelle for backup, but she was talking to Emily Jenkins, who had just put down her tray.

"Ava, relax," Zara said, "I'm just trying to help."

I sat there, frozen, while Zara bounded over to Chuck. I wanted to go after her, but it was like I was stuck to my chair. And the thing is, I wasn't even 100 percent sure if Zara was butting into my life to cause trouble, or if she was, as she put it, "trying to help." Does she meddle on purpose, or does she just not think about things? (Do I think *too much* about things?)

When Zara reached Chuck, he looked surprised. He was sitting with Aidan, Jamal, and Ethan (who are all good at sports), and she leaned in and started talking to him. Suddenly he turned and stared at me, wide-eyed. I wanted to disappear! Moments later, she bounded back. "He says he has to think about it," she reported and smiled as if she'd done me a favor!

Next Zara lowered her voice and asked, "Do either of you have a pad?"

I was about to say, "No!" but Maybelle said, "Let me check." And then (you won't believe this!) Maybelle dug into her backpack and unzipped a cosmetic case and handed Zara what I guessed was a little wrapped-up pad.

"Thanks," Zara said. "I'll be right back."

When she was gone, I said to Maybelle, "You got your period?!" She said no but that she and her mom had had a big talk, and her mom said that Maybelle might want to start carrying pads in case she or a friend ever needed them. Which I guess Zara did. (!!!)

"Whoa." I couldn't imagine ever having a conversation with my mom about that stuff—though maybe someday Pip will explain it all to me. Right now, whenever Mom and Pip talk about growing up, I just walk away.

I was also surprised Maybelle hadn't told me her mom had given her pads. We usually tell each other everything—even though some things take longer to come out than others.

"You and Zara are becoming pretty good friends," I mumbled because I couldn't bring myself to say, "Don't let her come between us!" or "I liked things the way they were!" or "You and I were friends first!" or "Why are you so nice to someone who keeps minding everybody *else's* business?"

Maybelle shrugged, and Zara came back, and we headed

toward class. I had to stop at my locker to get the rolled-up poster, and instead of waiting, they kept going, which made me feel even worse than before. I watched them walk away, and they were so close to each other that the sides of their backpacks bumped together.

Seconds later, I walked in and handed Mrs. Lemons the poster. I'd written the haiku in big, neat letters, and Pip had made the trees look like hands and the moon look like a shimmering golden ball.

Mrs. Lemons said she wanted to share my haiku with Mr. Ramirez and Mrs. White, the school librarian and the town librarian. I always think of Mrs. White as Mrs. (Bright) White, since she was Miss Bright before she married Mr. White. Mr. Ramirez, by the way, just got engaged to his boyfriend who teaches history at a private school. When he told us, everyone said, "Invite us to the wedding!!!" and he said he wished he could but it was going to be just family.

Anyway, Mrs. Lemons said that Mr. Ramirez and Mrs. (Bright) White had arranged for our fifth-grade classes to have a two-day writing workshop. She said that on January 26 and 29, Jerry Valentino, the children's author who had judged the library contest, was going to come with "writing tips and hands-on exercises."

I said, "Cool," even though that was the library contest that had gotten me into so much trouble.

Meanwhile, I had to find a seat. I looked around, but Maybelle and Zara were sitting together in front of Riley and the three

Emilys, and there were only two empty seats left. One was next to Chuck. Usually that would be fine, but he glanced at me then quickly looked away, which he never does. So I decided to sit by myself in the back.

I felt like I was in Siberia (wherever that is).

For a second, I wished we were all still in fourth grade, when we had assigned seats and rotating jobs like snack helper and line leader, and our teachers walked us everywhere, and we were the oldest in the school, and math wasn't hard, and friendships weren't fragile, and nobody ever tried to elbow her way into my life without an invitation.

AVA, ALL ALONE

P.S. I looked up Siberia. It's a freezing cold place on top of Russia. (Well, in *northern* Russia.)

1/7
AFTER DINNER

DEAR DIARY,

Pip and I just finished "L is for lionfish." Lionfish are beautiful but poisonous.

Zara is pretty and poisonous.

I was going to ~~confront~~ call Maybelle, but I thought, "What if she's *with* Zara?" so I didn't. (I changed "confront" to "call" because "confront" sounds unfriendly, and Maybelle is my friend.)

Mom brought home cat treats, a cat brush, and yellow tulips. Problem: When no one was looking, Taco nibbled at the tops of the tulips, so now all the petals have tiny bite marks.

(I thought it was cute, but Mom didn't.)

Taco let me brush him with the new brush and Mom kept me company and said that it's not easy training cats.

"What do you mean?" I asked.

"Most dogs can be bribed, but most cats can't," she said. "Can you picture a cat shaking or rolling over or playing dead?"

"I guess not," I admitted, but then told her the Aesop fable "The Thief and the Housedog," which goes something like this:

In the middle of the night, a thief came to break into a house. The housedog started barking and barking, so the thief tossed him two big, juicy steaks. But the dog was no fool. He said, "You can't bribe me! You're not my master and this is not my dinnertime. In fact, I'm going to bark louder than ever."

Mom smiled. "What's the moral?"

"If someone tries to bribe you, beware," I said.

Mom said that I could think of cat treats and dog biscuits as "rewards" and "incentives" and ways to "show love" and "encourage behavior modification"—and not just "bribes," since real bribes are bad and illegal. She also said that Dr. Gross's technicians often give pets treats after they squirt goo in their eyes or shove pills in their mouths or do procedures that are no fun.

It was nice talking to Mom, and inspiring too. In fact, I could feel myself coming up with a plan.

At dinner, we talked more about cat treats. Pip said she'd heard about a cat that got trained to use a toilet bowl instead of a litter box. Mom said toilet-training cats is challenging. Dad said potty-training *us* wasn't "a piece of cake" either. I said, "Can we change the subject?"

Dad laughed and taught us all a new word: ailurophobia. It means "fear of cats."

AVA, WHO IS NOT AILUROPHOBIC

1/8
BEFORE SCHOOL

Dear Diary,

Last night right before bed, I put my new plan into action. Even though cats are not easy to train, I thought Taco might be easy to *tempt.* I decided to try to lure him into my room using treats as bait. I was tired of Taco playing hard-to-get!

Remember how Dad used our paper mice to make a bee-line—a mouse line!—from my bedroom to his office? Well, after everyone had gone to bed, I opened the new bag of treats, spilled some into my hand, and placed them one by one in a line from the top of our stairs to the foot of my bed.

After I turned out my light, I tried to stay awake to see if Taco would come into my room. I even made believe I was on a safari in Africa. I pretended my bed was a jeep, and it was a moonlit night, and I was staying up late to spy a lion or leopard (or maybe a *pride* of lions or *leap* of leopards).

I kept my eyes peeled for as long as I could…but I must have fallen asleep.

I just woke up and guess what? Taco Cat is not in my room, and neither is the trail of treats! When no one was looking, he must have snuck in and eaten them all up, one by one!

Believe it or not, I consider this progress.

AVA THE ASTUTE

P.S. It's cool that cats can see in the dark—well, unless it's totally pitch-black.

1/8
Friday Night

Dear Diary,

The bonus words on today's spelling test were *catastrophe* and *cataclysmic*. Both start with *cat* and mean when something truly terrible happens.

Chuck used to tease me about all my 100s on spelling tests, but we haven't talked to each other since Zara talked to him about liking me. I know that's not a *cat*aclysmic *cat*astrophe, but it feels like one!

I miss our little looks. Like, whenever something funny happened, we used to look at each other. Today, when Riley said something about her horse, I wanted to sneak a peek at Chuck, but I knew I might feel dumb if he saw me looking at him. And what if he *didn't* see me looking because he *wasn't* looking back? That might feel even worse!

It didn't help that Maybelle and Zara were both wearing their string necklaces today and also matching sky-blue nail polish. I tried not to care, but I couldn't help but care, especially when I heard them giggle together. I started feeling sorry for myself, and then I started getting mad at myself for feeling sorry for myself.

It is *not* easy being eleven!

After school, I asked Maybelle if she wanted to sleep over. She said she had "plans." I mumbled, "Okay," but felt as if I'd swallowed an ice chip. I mean, if she had mathletes or a dentist appointment, she would have just said so. We stood there for an awkward moment and it was as if Zara were standing right between us.

I said "Bye" and walked home with Pip, and she made me work on *Alphabet Fish*. M was supposed to be for "minnow," but Pip wanted to change it to "mudskipper" because mudskippers have eyes that stick out on the top of their heads, like aliens, and she said they'd be more fun to draw. I said, "Whatever," because I didn't care whether M was for minnow, mudskipper, or...Moby Dick.

After a few minutes, I handed her a mudskipper rhyme and also:

N is for nurse shark.

If you were sick and this shark called nurse
Took care of you...you might get worse!

Confession: I was thinking of Zara when I wrote that. If Zara had never moved to Misty Oaks, she would never have moved in on my friendships with Maybelle and Chuck!

Is Taco my new friend? Maybe. But he could be a lot friendlier!

AVA, ALIENATED (THAT'S HOW IT CAN FEEL WHEN YOUR FRIENDS AREN'T BEING FRIENDLY.)

1/8
10:01 P.M.

Dear Diary,

You know how they say to think outside the box? Taco *pooped* outside the box.

And it was my fault!

We were watching TV and I used the downstairs bathroom. Afterward, I shut the door behind me and completely forgot that we're supposed to leave it open so Taco can go in and out and use his litter box whenever he wants. Just now I remembered that I'd closed that bathroom door *hours* ago! I went down to open the door but…too late! There were two little poops right next to the door. Cat scat! (Scat is a fancy way to say P-O-O-P—or poo or doo or dung or manure or feces or excrement.)

Poor Taco! He'd obviously tried to be a good boy! He could have pooped *anywhere*. And cats prefer to bury their P-O-O-P and not leave it out in the open for everyone to see.

I got a bunch of toilet paper, picked up the poops, dropped them into the toilet, and flushed.

I'm glad Taco didn't pee outside the box. That would have been way harder to clean up.

Cleaning up the P-O-O-P was surprisingly easy—not that I want to go into the pooper-scooper business.

Here's what I've been thinking: Most dogs are trainable and protective and loyal and friendly and fun to take on walks (which is good). But when you take your dog on a walk, you have to take a plastic bag with you and deal with the doody (not good). You're expected to just *stand* there while your dog is crouching and straining as though it's nothing. And neither you, nor your dog, are supposed to act embarrassed even though you're in public. If your dog has diarrhea, you're still supposed to clean it up. And if there's no garbage can in sight, well, you're supposed to just carry the P-O-O-P (or diarrhea!) around in your plastic bag until you find one.

Yuck!!

I think cats are more dignified—but then, I'm more of a cat person than a dog person.

AVA, CAT ~~PERSON~~ KID

P.S. I was brushing my teeth and left the water running. Taco jumped up, stuck his head under the faucet, and starting lapping at the water. It was cute. But it was *not* dignified!

P.P.S. I'll admit that if a stranger wanted to break into your house, a dog might be a handier pet than a cat. Like, there are *watchdogs*, but no *watchcats*. A dog might also be handier if you accidentally spilled food on the floor.

1/9
Saturday N-O-O-N

Dear Diary,

Dad made a big Irish breakfast: eggs, bacon, sausage, baked beans, mushrooms, tomatoes, and scones.

I asked Maybelle to come over, but she had "stuff to do." She said I should come over Monday after school.

Monday feels far away, but I said, "Okay," and decided that that's when I'd ask her what Zara has been saying about me.

Mom just took clean clothes out of the dryer to fold, and when the laundry pile was all toasty warm, Taco hopped on top and settled in with his legs tucked under him. He looked like a hen sitting on eggs and seemed pleased with himself.

Mom and I smiled as if we were sharing an inside joke. I was glad Mom didn't shoo Taco away or make a remark about cat fur on clean clothes. She even turned to Taco and said in a singsongy voice I'd never heard before, "Are you finally making yourself at home? Yes, you are. Yes, you are."

It was sweet, to tell you the truth.

Ava and Taco at Home

1/10

DEAR DIARY,

Dad and I were making Sunday sundaes, and I told him I wished Taco would jump on my bed and snuggle with me and purr.

Dad said, "Be patient. Rome wasn't built in a day."

I was about to ask, "How many days was it built in?" but instead said, "He's had *ten* days!"

"And he *is* warming up to us," Dad pointed out. We both looked at Taco. He'd found a patch of sunshine on the kitchen floor and was grooming himself: licking his five-toed paws and "brushing" his mismatched ears.

He might have sensed that we were talking about him because he lifted his head and looked right at me.

"Who's a good boy?" I said and got on the floor and puckered up as if to give him a kiss. He sniffed my lips and sneezed a little cat sneeze. That made Dad laugh—and *that* made Taco scamper off.

Since Maybelle was (supposedly) busy, Pip and I texted Bea to see if she wanted to come over. She texted, "Can Ben come too?" Pip liked that idea, so we texted back, "Sure."

Now Bea and Ben are *both* about to walk in. Pip is nervous, I can tell. She just put on lip gloss. Lip gloss! Next thing you know, she'll be wearing eyeliner! Or cologne!

She has also been cleaning her room. She said she's almost done.

I said "almost" is an unusual word because all its letters are in alphabetical order.

I also said that my initials are in alphabetical order and hers aren't.

She said, "Who cares?" I said that if my first name were her *middle* name, she'd be Pip Ava Wren and her initials would be P. A. W.—like "paw." She rolled her eyes as if she had way more important things to think about—like brushing her hair and getting ready for you-know-who.

A. E. W.

1/10
Sunday Night

Dear Diary,

There wasn't enough snow to make snowmen, so Pip, Ben, Bea, and I made snowkids. Pip and Ben kept making happy faces at each other, and their gloves kept touching. Well, Pip and Ben's snowboy turned out way cuter than Bea's and my snowgirl. Pip can draw *and* sculpt! At the last minute, I said they should give their snowboy freckles, so they dotted him with Apple Jacks. Unfortunately, the "freckles" looked like chicken pox. (Fortunately, no one blamed me.)

Back inside, we all made hot chocolate and ate peanuts. (We aren't allowed to have peanuts in school, so we always stock up at home.) Pip showed Bea and Ben *Alphabet Fish*—because she's proud of it and we're up to "P is for porcupine fish." We also talked about Meow Meow, Taco Cat, and even long-lost Goldy Lox. It was fun talking to an eighth-grade boy.

Ben told us a joke he'd heard:

Question: What's the difference between a dog and a cat?

Answer: When a dog has a wonderful master who feeds him and grooms him and cleans up after him, the dog thinks, "He must be

God!" But when a cat has a wonderful master who feeds him and grooms him and cleans up after him, the cat thinks, "I must be God!"

We laughed, and then Pip went to play a computer game in the living room.

Bea and I went to the kitchen, and I put my hot chocolate cup in the sink and said, "Bea, can I ask you for advice?" Bea is the only person I know who wants to be an advice columnist when she grows up.

"If it's about Taco," she said, "I don't have any Pet Pointers. I know some cute cat videos though. And we stock tons of cat books at the shop because Americans own, like, a hundred million cats."

"It's not about Taco," I said, a lump in my throat. "You know that new fifth-grade girl, Zara?" Bea listened, and I told her that Maybelle was always busy with Zara, and that Zara had asked Chuck about me, and now things were awkward between us.

"I think you and Maybelle will always be friends," Bea said reassuringly. "And with Chuck, maybe if you try to act the way you used to, things will go back to how they were." I didn't say anything, so she added, "It might feel forced at first, but no one ever died of awkwardness."

I nodded, remembering when she'd told Pip that no one ever died of awkwardness. Who knew *I'd* be asking Bea for advice months later?

Taco Cat pitter-pattered in and rubbed against our shins. I think he was actually inviting us to pet him.

"You know what Taco likes?" I said. "To be brushed."

I got out his brush, and Bea and I took turns brushing him.

"Meow Meow loves when we brush him. He purrs up a storm."

"Taco never purrs," I said.

"Really?" Bea looked surprised.

"Well, not yet anyway. He's very independent. Even for a cat."

"Meow Meow is the opposite. She's very affectionate—but a little needy sometimes." Bea smiled. "We don't mind though."

I didn't think I would mind either. (I mean *I'm* a little needy sometimes!)

Ava, Whose Cat Does Not Purr

P.S. Is having a cat that doesn't purr like having a dog that doesn't wag its tail? Will he ever purr? And will he ever realize that I don't even want to be his master—just his *friend*?

P.P.S. Bea and I went on Dad's computer, and she showed me an amazing video of a cat playing Jenga. I think the cat was gifted or something.

1/11 (PALINDROME DATE)
IN BED

DEAR DIARY,

After school, I went to Maybelle's—just me. It started out fun. We made popcorn (P-O-P-P-O-P-P-O-P) and played Slow Down/ Speed Up. It's the game when one person starts doing something, whether it's jumping jacks or juggling marshmallows, and the other says, "Slow down!" or "Speed up!" The person has to do whatever she's doing really slowwwwly or lightning fast. When Carmen or Lucia play it with us, they say, *"¡Más lento!"* or *"¡Más rápido!"* And in the summer, we sometimes go outside and do slow and fast cartwheels.

Today, I was happy to be playing with just Maybelle (and not Zara). We started making necklaces with her beads, but after a while, I couldn't hold in my questions anymore. So I asked straight out: "Did Zara say anything about me, like, behind my back?"

Maybelle looked guilty and as if she didn't know if she should answer.

Which was an answer right there.

"What did she say?" I pressed.

Maybelle folded her legs up and put her chin on her knee.

I could tell she didn't want to report their conversations, but maybe I was sort of cornering her.

She sighed, and we both looked at our beads instead of at each other. "She thinks," Maybelle finally began in a quiet voice, "that you're kind of a teachers' pet."

My mouth flopped open. Even though that may not be untrue (which is a double negative), it was *not* what I expected to hear.

Still, I decided I could live with that. I mean, it's a fact that Mrs. Lemons likes me. And I like her back. But for what it's worth, not *all* teachers think I'm special. I annoy Miss Hamshire. She acts like I'm bad at math on purpose.

Well, it turned out that Maybelle wasn't done! While I was contemplating Zara's first complaint, Maybelle came up with a second.

"Zara also says that your primary topic of conversation is your cat."

That made me mad! Of course I talk a lot about Taco Cat! I was desperate for a cat, then I got one, and we've had him only eleven days! What does Zara expect me to talk about? Carpet cleaners? Climate change?

I was trying to decide whether to defend myself when Maybelle said that Zara also wonders why I haven't let her meet Taco yet.

What?!?

"I haven't *stopped* her from meeting him," I said.

"She says you've never once invited her over even though she helped make the paper mice."

I wanted to shout, "Oh puh-lease! Zara doesn't have the right to jump feetfirst into my whole life!" But I didn't. I just mumbled, "She can meet him."

"Now?" Maybelle asked, which made *me* feel sort of cornered.

I shrugged and said, "I guess." Then I wished I hadn't, because suddenly Maybelle was speed-dialing Zara and inviting her to hang out at my house! Next thing you know, Maybelle's mom was driving Maybelle and me to my house and picking up Zara on the way as though that had been the plan all along! I couldn't believe it!!

Even Dad looked surprised when he opened the door and there we were, all three of us. We walked in and searched all over for Taco and finally found him sleeping in the corner of Mom's closet, by the slippers.

Zara said he was handsome.

I said that cats spend most of the day sleeping—about eighteen hours.

Maybelle said, "That's three-fourths of the day! Humans sleep only one-third of the day." That was a very Maybelle thing to say. (She can do fractions in her head.)

Zara said that sloths sleep even more. "They sleep more than any other animal in the animal kingdom."

Zara had brought a ping-pong ball for Taco to play with, and he chased it around and even let her pet him. At first, I thought Taco was being a traitor. But I told myself not to feel that way. The problem though, is that it's hard not to feel whatever you're feeling, even when you try to talk yourself out of it.

Taco wanted to keep playing, and he pressed his little white zigzag against Zara's shin. She laughed and said, "He's giving me a head butt!" For a second, I thought she was calling my cat a butthead! Then I realized that this was in *my* head.

Anyway, Maybelle said that in 1963, France sent the first cat ever into outer space. "Her name was Felicette."

"Really?" I said.

"Oui," Maybelle said. "A lot of animals went into space. Dogs, monkeys, mice, turtles, even newts and fruit flies."

"Newts?" Zara and I said at the exact same time.

She gave me a little smile so I went ahead and gave her a little smile back, which was nice of me. Then we both said "Jinx" at the same time.

"Did the cat live?" I asked Maybelle.

Maybelle said the cat went up for fifteen minutes and "came back famous."

Zara said, "Cool." She was petting Taco and he was letting her. "What a good cat," she said. I appreciated her appreciation, even though I was glad Taco did not choose that moment to purr. But then Zara said something I did *not* appreciate. She said, "I wonder who he used to belong to."

"What do you mean?" I said. Obviously, I think of Taco as *mine*, not as some hand-me-down stray.

"I mean, did you look for Lost Cat signs?"

"No..." I said and wondered whether we should have.

"My stepfather once had a dog that got lost," Zara continued. "But it had tags, and we put up signs, and the person who found him gave him back."

"Taco didn't have tags and we didn't see any signs," I stated in a way that I hoped made it clear that this conversation was over.

Soon Maybelle and Zara left, and I felt irritated that Zara had come over at all. I hugged Taco close and was glad that he was mine, and that he's Taco *Wren*—not Taco Smith or Taco Jones or even Taco Bell!

Ava Elle Wren, Owner of Taco Cat Wren

P.S. Dinner was a revolting concoction of kale, quinoa, and mushrooms. Ugh! Why can't we have Taco Tuesdays instead of Meatless Mondays?

1/12
BARELY AWAKE

DEAR DIARY,

I had the scariest dream!

A gigantic elephant was trying to barge into my room. I locked the door, but the elephant started getting in anyway. I was really scared and didn't know where to hide, and I hoped it would not get in and trample or squash me!

When I woke up, I thought: What the heck was that about? Had I read something scary before bed? Was my nightmare inspired by an Aesop fable about elephants?

But no, I hadn't. And I doubt Aesop wrote about elephants in ancient Greece.

I doubt Basho wrote about elephants in ancient Japan either.

My mind was all over the place, and then I remembered the expression "an elephant in the room," which means the upsetting thing no one is talking about.

Right now what's upsetting me is what Zara said about Lost Cat signs. I have to admit: it didn't even occur to me to look for Lost Cat signs—let alone round up my friends to make Found Cat signs. And even if I *had* made Found Cat signs, I probably wouldn't have posted them in plain sight. I would have posted them in closets and behind doors!

Should I talk to Mom or Dad about this?

I wish Zara had kept her mouth zipped!

Ava, Angry

1/13
BEDTIME

DEAR DIARY,

Question: What if someone out there *is* looking for Taco Cat?

I don't even want to think about that.

I could think about Chuck, but he and I haven't said a word to each other in six days.

I could think about Maybelle because she's coming over again tomorrow. But what if Zara thinks she's invited? She isn't!

Sometimes I wish I could just turn off my brain.

AVA, AGITATED

1/14
4:11

Dear Diary,

Maybelle came over, and Dad built us a fire in the fireplace while we made banana milk. That's when we put bananas and ice cream and ice in a blender. (Taco hates when we use the blender.) We also made a snack of banana slices topped with dabs of chunky peanut butter. (Dad and Mom both bought bananas so we have way too many.) Anyway, Maybelle and I took off our shoes and warmed our toes by the fire, and I decided to tell her that I'd been worrying.

"About what?"

"About what Zara said about Lost Cat signs and also"—my voice caught—"about Zara wanting to steal you away." I looked into the fire, which was crackly and smoky-smelling and yellow-orange with a little blue and purple too. Then I looked at Maybelle and added softly, "I don't want you to dump me."

"Ava, I would never dump you," Maybelle said. She sounded a teeny tiny bit annoyed. "And I didn't get mad last fall when you started spending time with Bea."

"True," I said, feeling embarrassed and bite-size.

"Besides, didn't you once tell me that Bea said people can't *steal* friends, they can only *make* friends?"

"Yes," I admitted, impressed that Maybelle remembered.

"Zara is new," she continued, "and it seemed like she could use a friend. And you weren't around much because you had just gotten Taco."

I nodded, trying to be understanding, but I still wished Zara hadn't zeroed in on *my* BFF. "Doesn't Zara ever get on your nerves?" I asked. "She says really random things."

"Everyone says random things," Maybelle said, and it occurred to me that while Zara can be insensitive, maybe I can be *over*sensitive. "And you don't have to like her just because I like her."

"I don't *hate* her..." I said quietly. "But I like when it's just us."

Taco Cat came padding over and I reached down to pet him. Instead of running away, he stayed still. I went to get his brush, and Maybelle and I took turns brushing him and brushing him.

You are *not* going to believe what happened next!

Brace yourself because this is BIG!

Taco Cat was lying there, letting us brush him by the fire for like, three minutes, and then, out of the blue, I heard a rhythmic sound, a soft gentle *rumble bumble rumble bumble*. It was coming from *him*! He was purring!

And purring!!

And purring!!!

He remembered that he had a little purring motor inside him, and he turned it on!

Maybelle and I kept brushing him, and we kept looking at each other and smiling.

"It's the first time he's ever purred!" I whispered. "I'm glad you're here with me."

"Me too," she whispered back. "You think purring is how cats say, 'I feel happy'?"

"Or 'I feel safe'?" I said.

"Or 'Thank you'?" she said.

"Or 'I love you'?" We kept brushing and brushing, and Taco kept purring and purring. "My mom said cats also communicate by blinking. It's their way of blowing a kiss."

"Don't some cats communicate by killing mice and birds and leaving them on doorsteps as tokens of affection?"

"Do they?" I asked, horrified.

"Maybe not in winter," Maybelle said.

Taco kept purring away, and I hoped he would never bring me a dead mouse or chickadee valentine.

"Some big cats purr too," I said. "Lions and tigers roar, but cheetahs and pumas purr."

"Zara's pet guinea pig used to purr," Maybelle said.

We kept listening to Taco Cat's *rumble bumble rumble bumble*, and I was glad that Maybelle was *here* to *hear* it (homonym alert), even if she did bring up Zara.

It's funny how some big events really are newsworthy. Like when rockets go into space, or athletes beat world records, or presidents get elected.

But some big events are kind of small. Like when your cat

comes out in the open or finally purrs. Or when a shy person opens up like a flower bud. Or when two best friends clear the air.

Later, as Maybelle was putting on her winter coat to go home, she said, "Ava, Zara is my new friend, but you're my old friend and my best friend. And that's a much bigger deal."

AVA, A #1

1/15
BEFORE SCHOOL

DEAR DIARY,

I'm glad Maybelle and I talked yesterday. And maybe Zara really did need a friend. Like Taco did. And maybe Maybelle needed someone to talk to about bras and growing-up stuff, especially since she doesn't have a sister and it's possible that I have been a teeny tiny itty bitty eensy weensy bit cat-consumed.

Zara doesn't have sisters or brothers either. She never even talks about her parents—just her grandparents.

I am trying to be mature about everything—which is not particularly easy. (Maturity may not be my strong suit.)

By the way, Pip got jealous that Taco purred for Maybelle, and not her, so I told her that next time Taco settles under a lamp or by the fire or in a spot of sunshine, she should tiptoe over and brush him softly. (Usually, Pip and Taco play runaround games. She chases him around the living room or they play a game we call Bat and Bite. It's when Pip jiggles a ribbon and Taco bats it and bites it!)

Last night, I let Pip feed Taco. We'd gone to the Great Wall for dinner (the squid came with tentacles, yuck!), and when we came home, I forgot to feed Taco. It was the first time that ever happened! Well, he rubbed my shins and also gently bit my ankle to remind me, but by then I was upstairs and about to get in bed, so I told Pip she could feed him. Pip was happy, and this morning, she told me that when Taco heard her open the bag, he came running!

Here are three sounds Taco loves:

1. A can of cat food being opened
2. A bag of cat food being shaken
3. A bag of cat treats coming out of the R-E-W-A-R-D-D-R-A-W-E-R

Here are four sounds Taco hates:

1. Dad grinding coffee
2. Mom using her hair dryer
3. Me using the blender
4. Mom or Dad vacuuming

AVA, AWARE AND OBSERVANT

P.S. We got fortune cookies after dinner. Pip's said, "You have a yearning for perfection." Mine said… well, I'll tape it here:

Declare peace every day.

1/15
AFTER SCHOOL

DEAR DIARY,

In the library, Mr. Ramirez said he liked my cat and moon haiku, and that when Jerry Valentino comes to our school in ten days, a reporter from the town newspaper, the *Misty Oaks Monitor*, is going to "cover" the workshop.

"Cover?"

"Write about it," he explained, then added, "Zara said you and your sister have been working on a picture book called *Something Fishy.*"

"*Alphabet Fish*," I corrected, only half-surprised that Zara had blabbed about—and retitled—our book.

But for once, maybe it was good that Zara had meddled, because I blurted, "Do you think Mr. Valentino could *critique* it?" I'd never used that word, but it was a bonus word on today's spelling test. It means to "evaluate or read critically."

"Maybe..." Mr. Ramirez said, taken aback. "Is it short?"

That was funny because that's always the first thing I want to know about a book. "It's mostly pictures," I said.

"I don't see why not," he said. "It wouldn't be fair to ask him to read a student novel, but a short book, sure."

"We haven't quite finished."

"Can you have it ready by next Friday?"

"Yes," I said even though I didn't know how
to a deadline.

"Don't sacrifice quality for speed," he cautioned.

"We won't," I said. And then, even though I haven't been all that into *Alphabet Fish* lately, I started daydreaming. I was giving the book to Mr. Ramirez, who was giving it to Mr. Valentino, who was giving it to an agent, who was giving it to an editor, who was giving it to a publisher, who was giving it to the factory people who turn floppy pages into hardcover books, who were giving it to librarians and bookstore owners and reviewers and bloggers who were all telling regular readers about it. In my mind, our ABC book was on its way to being a bestseller! In my mind, Pip and I were about to be a world-famous writer-artist sister duo!

I tried to remind myself of the Aesop moral: "Don't count your chickens before they are hatched." But it was hard not to start counting. In fact, I started picturing a basket of eggs and a half dozen baby chicks hatching out of shells, their tiny beaks first, *peep peep peep*, *cheep cheep cheep*.

One two three
four five six...
Chick chick chick
chicks chicks chicks...

Ava Ignoring Aesop

1/15
BEDTIME

DEAR DIARY,

I told Pip that Mr. Ramirez said he would give our book to Jerry. I even mentioned that we might turn into a world-famous author-illustrator team.

"Dream on, Ava," Pip said, but I bet she has been daydreaming too. She once told me that while she would *not* want to be famous, she *would* like to be an artist.

I handed her:

Q is for queen triggerfish.

The queen triggerfish is big and bright;
It changes colors and sleeps at night.

Then I casually mentioned that we had to finish by next Friday.

"What??!" Pip said, her voice rising. "Ava, we still have ten letters to go!" She was freaking out, but I think she was also getting extra inspired because next thing you know, she was drawing an elaborate border of shiny golden crowns for the Q page and telling me to get to work on "rainbow trout."

I am now going to bed. I'm going to leave my door wide open in case Taco Cat decides to visit. Lately, when Pip and I have been writing or drawing, he'll plunk himself on top of our picture book as if asking to be petted—or maybe saying, "I dare you to make me move."

Pip says it's annoying. Me, I never mind putting down my pen and picking up my cat. I love that he's becoming more affectionate!

AVA, AFFECTIONATE

P.S. Chuck and I have gone over a week without talking. Bea said I should try to act normal with him, but how can I when we haven't been sitting next to each other? Is he avoiding me? (Or does he...*miss* me a little too?) I can't believe Zara caused so much trouble with one stupid question! Arrrggghh!

1/16
Saturday N-O-O-N

Dear Diary,

Here are my latest poems:

S is for seahorse.

With a kangaroo's pouch and a horse's head,
The dad carries the babies and makes sure they're fed.

and

T is for trumpetfish.

The slow trumpetfish is straight as a stick,
Hiding in branches is its very best trick.

Speaking of hiding, Taco Cat isn't hiding as much as he used to—except when he finds a bag or box or wants to take a catnap. It seems like he'd rather keep us company than keep his distance. When we watch a movie on TV, for instance, he'll sit near us, almost as if he's watching too.

Sometimes he even follows us into the bathroom. (This morning I heard Pip say, "Taco, get out! I need privacy!")

When Mom or Dad drives into our garage, or Pip comes home from art class, Taco pricks up his ears and goes trotting over to the back door to say a quiet hello.

He doesn't like when we play Boggle though. When anyone shakes the letters, he takes off. So that's another sound he abhors. (And "abhors," which means "hates," is another six-letter word with all its letters in alphabetical order.)

Personally, I think Taco can't really change his inner nature, which is that he is a bit of a scaredy-cat.

I wonder if Zara can't change her inner nature either, which is that she's a bit of a blabbermouth.

I once read an Aesop fable about how it's hard to hide your inner nature. It's called "The Cat and the Maiden," and it goes like this:

The gods were arguing about whether a living creature can change its nature. Jupiter, the king of the gods, said yes, but Venus, the goddess of love, said no. To prove his point, Jupiter turned a cat into a beautiful maiden. A man fell madly in love with her and proposed. At the wedding, Jupiter said to Venus, "Look how lovely she is. Who would have thought that she used to be a cat?" Venus said, "Watch this!" and tossed a squeaky mouse into her path. No sooner did the bride see it, than she pounced upon it. The groom was horrified! And Venus said to Jupiter, "See? You can't change who you are."

Well, not to argue with Aesop or anything, but I don't agree that you are who you are. Maybe in *some* ways. But not in all ways. I mean, I think people and cats *can* change a little bit, if they want to and they try.

Like, Pip and Taco are both a lot less timid than they used to be. Right now, Pip is at Isabel's, and Pip never used to go to other kids' houses. As for Taco, maybe he will always seem aloof and like he's planning his escape. But he is settling down a bit and trusting us. And I'll say this: his ready-to-run personality makes his "cat cuddles" extra sweet. >^. .^<

AVA, NOT ALOOF

1/16
BEFORE DINNER

DEAR DIARY,

Dad and I were in the car running errands, and I asked him if we should have put up Found Cat signs.

"Ava, we didn't *find* Taco. We *adopted* Taco."

I told him that Zara had asked if I knew who Taco belonged to before us.

Dad patted my knee. "I doubt Taco thinks he ever belonged to anyone. I bet he thinks *we* belong to him. We're the ones who feed him, right?" I nodded. "Maybe he thinks *he* owns us!"

We talked about how pets aren't property, and I told him Ben's jokes about cats versus dogs. Dad told me that in ancient Egypt, cats were revered as gods, mostly because they killed the mice and rats that were spreading disease and eating up all the grain.

AVA, OWNED BY TACO GOD

P.S. Maybelle is coming for a sleepover. Y-A-Y! First time in a long time!!

1/17
1:17

Dear Diary,

Maybelle brought a laser light with her. It made a red beam, and Taco chased it everywhere, even up walls. (We were careful not to flash it in his eyes.)

Pip was in the kitchen illustrating the V rhyme she made me write:

V is for viperfish.

The viperfish has sharp teeth and shines its own light,
It swims deep down by day but less deep at night.

Pip is worried that we won't finish in time, but after dinner, I told her to come outside with Maybelle and me, and she did. The three of us bundled up and went to look at the stars. Maybelle started talking about life in outer space and that French space cat. I said that in science we learned about "inherited, acquired, and learned" traits. For instance, if Taco hadn't had certain private parts snipped off, he could have had kittens, and some of his kittens *might* have been taco-colored (inherited), but none of them would have been born with a bitten-up ear (acquired) or able to play Jenga (learned).

This morning, Taco found a diamond of sunlight and lay down on his side. Maybelle joked that it was a "rhombus" of sunlight and said he looked like "a breaded pork chop." That made me laugh, but I have to admit that if Zara had said the exact same thing, I might have wanted to punch her face. (Not that I would have.)

I said that when Taco sits with his paws tucked in, he looks like a golden loaf of bread.

The twins came over (wearing orange sweatshirts), and we played Slow Down/Speed Up. Pip and Maybelle were eating cereal, and when Carmen said, "*¡Más lento!*" they lifted their spoons in slow motion, and when she said, "*¡Más rápido!*" they shoveled cereal into their mouths, spoonful after spoonful. It was funny—but I was glad Mom and Dad weren't watching.

Sometimes I wish I really could slow down time because I like being a kid. Especially when everyone is getting along.

Does *growing* up mean *growing* pains?

Actually, I think Pip likes being thirteen more than she liked being my age, eleven. She used to be moodier and more *temperamental* (a hard bonus word because of the "a" between "temper" and "mental"). Now she's happier—which is better for her and for us. But she still has her moments! And she's been stressing about finishing the fish book on time.

Taco was sitting in the living room with his left paw stretched out in front of him. Maybelle said, "He looks like the king of the beasts."

I said, "Or the prince of the beasts."

Lucia asked, "Has he purred yet?"

Pip said, "Yes! For me and Ava and Maybelle!"

We told Carmen and Lucia to go up to him very slowly and brush him very gently. And sure enough, instead of bolting, Taco let them brush him. After a long, long while, he even turned on his *rumble bumble rumble bumble* motor and started purring and vibrating. Lucia pressed her ears against his side and he didn't run away!

"Más rápido," Lucia whispered, and then, *"Más lento."* But Taco didn't speed up or slow down. He kept purring at his very own speed.

Ava, Whose Cat is Purrrrrfect

1/17
TWO HOURS LATER
IN DR. GROSS'S WAITING ROOM

Dear Diary,

I'm really worried about Taco!! After Maybelle and the twins went home, Dad and Pip went to a matinee, and I noticed that Taco started acting strange. His bathroom door was open, and he was going in and out and in and out. He was also crouching as if he had to pee but couldn't. His little behind was all quivery, and he looked at me with his big round eyes and gave a melancholy meow as if to tell me something was wrong. It seemed like he was even trying to pee *outside* his litter box, which he never does.

I went into the bathroom and saw a couple of tiny pink drops on the white bath mat. I didn't want to get Taco in trouble, but I thought I'd better tell Mom.

But she wasn't home! I remembered that she'd gone out for a walk with our neighbor, Mrs. Farris. I called Mom on her cell phone, but then I heard her phone buzzing in her purse—she'd left it on the kitchen counter!

Taco looked up at me—but not with a love-blink, more like an anxious expression. I was trying to figure out what to do—stay with him or get help—and decided to put on my coat and boots and run to the park and find Mom.

At first I couldn't find her anywhere. Then I saw her way ahead, so I ran and ran and caught up to her.

Mom seemed surprised to see me. I told her about Taco, and I don't know what I expected her to say, but I did not expect her to say, "Ava, we need to get Taco to the clinic *immediately*."

"But it's Sunday!"

"Let's hurry home. I'll call Dr. Gross, and you get the cat carrier. We have no time to lose!"

We said good-bye to Mrs. Farris and ran back. Mom called Dr. Gross, and I got Taco into his carrier and held him on my lap as Mom drove. Mom and I both kept telling Taco things like, "Don't be scared," and "Dr. Gross is going to take care of you."

Now we're at the clinic, which would normally be closed. If regular people have a Sunday emergency, they have to drive to the animal hospital twenty-five minutes away. But Dr. Gross told Mom he'd meet us here.

It's strange to be sitting in the empty waiting room. It's hardly ever empty. Mom said I could watch the "procedure," but I was afraid to. I knew it would be better for me to write in you.

Writing always helps.

I'm actually writing with the "magic pen" Dad gave me, the silver one from the Dublin Writers Museum in Ireland, the one I almost lost. I barely use it anymore because I don't want to lose it again. But I grabbed it for luck, just in case.

Taco may need all the luck he can get!
Why is it taking so, *so* long? I don't like this!

Ava, Agonizing

1/17
BACK HOME WITHOUT TACO!

DEAR DIARY,

Poor Taco Cat has to stay at the vet's *without* us! He's back in a cage! On the drive home, Mom said that because there was blood in his pee, they have to be sure he doesn't have a "urethral obstruction" which can be "extremely serious in a male cat."

Mom always sounds different when she talks about animals.

She said Dr. Gross remembered Taco because of his "distinctive coloration" and the "lacerations" on his ear. He gave him an "antibiotic injection," "anti-inflammatory medication," and anesthesia. And Taco conked out, which meant that at least he couldn't feel anything. Mom said Dr. Gross did a "bladder radiograph" and "urine analysis" and blood tests too, because he had a UTI.

"UTI?"

"Urinary tract infection," Mom said.

"Is that bad?" I asked.

Mom looked somber. "In some cats, it can be fatal, but I think Taco is going to pull through just fine."

"I'm scared," I said.

"I know," Mom said.

"Is Taco going to be okay?" I whispered.

"I hope so," Mom said, even though I'd wanted her to say, "Yes, of course!" She added, "Dr. Gross is an excellent vet."

I nodded but felt like sobbing. "Is this all going to cost a lot?" I asked. I don't even know why I asked except that Mom and Dad sometimes worry about money, so I sometimes do too.

"Dr. Gross will give us a discount," Mom said. We were quiet for a moment, then she said, "You know what else he told me?"

"What?"

"He thinks having a pet has been good for me because it's given me a greater understanding of how our clients feel when they have an emergency or an end-of-life decision."

"We don't have an end-of-life decision!"

"No, I don't think we do." Mom took another peek at me even though she was driving. "But I guess I never fully understood how *attached* people get to their pets. I never had a pet growing up."

"I know," I said, then added, "I'm sorry," because I felt sad for Mom-when-she-was-a-girl.

"I really *did* want a Dalmatian puppy," Mom admitted. "My best friend's dog had a litter, and she wanted to give me one." Mom smiled a soft, sad smile. "You know, when I first started working at the clinic, I was surprised by how much everyone talks to the animals."

"What do you mean?"

"Like, just now, Dr. Gross said, 'Don't worry, Taco. You'll be your old self again soon.'"

"*You* talk to Taco."

"I know. But I never thought I would."

It was nice talking to Mom in the dark car. "When will we know for sure that we don't have an end-of-life decision?" I kind of wanted a guarantee.

"Ava, you did everything right. Taco let you know that something was wrong, and you let me know, and I let Dr. Gross know. Everything's going to be okay."

"Promise?"

"I can't promise."

"Mom, you know how cats have nine lives?" My voice cracked. "What if Taco has already used his all up?"

We were turning into our driveway, and I hated that he wasn't with us. I pictured him on the arm of the sofa, pricking up his ears, hearing our car, and heading over to greet us at the door. "Think about it!" I said. "He got attacked by a coyote, *and* he had a peeing problem—that's *two* lives in *three* weeks! What if, when he was a kitten, he fell off a roof, or picked a fight with a raccoon, or—?"

Mom drove into our garage and parked. Then she opened her arms and gave me a hug. For most moms, that's probably no big deal, but my mom is not very huggy. It's not part of her inner nature. Her mom, Nana Ethel, doesn't hug at all. She gives stiff little pat-pats that are the *opposite* of bear hugs.

I hugged Mom back and wondered if, as Dr. Gross said, Taco really was softening her up. I also wondered this: If Goldy Lox had died *now* instead of two years ago, would things have been different? Would Mom have let us give him a proper burial in the backyard instead of flushing him down the toilet?

Well, "what's done, is done," I thought, which was me quoting Dad quoting Shakespeare.

Mom and I walked in, and Dad and Pip were right there ~~dying~~ wanting to know everything. (I can't believe I wrote "dying"!!)

Mom told them that Taco had been "straining to urinate" and that I had done "everything right." She said we'd get test results soon and, if all went well, we'd get Taco back tomorrow. We'd have to give him medication and "modify his diet" and get him to drink more water. Mom said it's good Taco likes to drink from faucets since our house is heated and the air gets so dry in winter.

I asked Dad if he knew where the expression "nine lives" comes from.

He said no, but that Shakespeare used it in *Romeo and Juliet.* Then Dad found the exact lines and showed them to me (which was *very* Dad). They were in a fight scene when Romeo's friend Mercutio calls his enemy, "Good King of Cats" and says he wants one of his "nine lives."

Anyway, I hope Taco stays fast asleep at Dr. Gross's. If he wakes up in a cage, he'll be so scared. (My bigger hope is that he wakes up!)

Poor Taquito! (That's Pip's nickname for him—she says that in Spanish, adding "ito" means "little.")

AVA WITHOUT TACO

1/17
AN HOUR LATER

DEAR DIARY,

Pip said we should do another page to distract ourselves. I didn't want to, but Pip seemed upset and I didn't feel like fighting with her. So I wrote a W rhyme and handed it over:

W is for witch flounder.

Some witches have cats, ride brooms, and cast spells.
These witches are fish that swim among shells.

Pip is now drawing a border with Halloween cats and witches on brooms. She's also revising the borders from the early pages. Dad says writers have to do revisions ("Write and rewrite till you get it right!"), and I guess artists do too.

I could do revisions on my earlier fish poems, but number one, I don't feel like it, and number two, Pip already illustrated them the way they are.

I'm glad Mom told me not to worry, but I can't help but

worry. I wish Taco were here! The house feels so empty without him!

AVA, ANXIOUS

1/17
MIDDLE OF THE NIGHT

DEAR DIARY,

An X rhyme just came to me so I turned on the penlight Bea gave me and am writing it down:

X marks the spot where the fish swam away.
What was it? Sunfish? Starfish? Moonfish? Moray?

X-O-X

A-V-A

1/18
RIGHT BEFORE SCHOOL

DEAR DIARY,

I gave Pip my middle-of-the-night masterpiece, but she said X has to stand for a fish, not a spot. I said that she could draw wavy water and make a border of suns and stars and moons. She said she did not want a page without fish in the middle of a fish book. I said, "Why not? It'd be funny." She said, "I just don't!"

Well, instead of making a new X poem, I felt like making a giant X on Pip's artwork.

I felt like shouting, "I'm sick of fish and I'm sick of collaborating, and you'll be lucky if I even write the last three rhymes!"

But I didn't feel like starting World War III, so I dashed off an "X is for x-ray tetra" poem and handed it to her. I'm *not* going to copy it in here because it's not very good and the whole thing makes me mad.

AVA, ANNOYED AND ARGUMENTATIVE BUT ATTEMPTING TO BE ADULT

P.S. Are Pip and I both in X-tra bad moods because we're worried about Taco?

1/18
RIGHT AFTER SCHOOL

DEAR DIARY,

Taco is back!! Dad picked him up while we were at school. Taco must have missed us too because he started purring the second I hugged him and kissed his little snout! Poor Taco! Was he afraid he would never get to see us again? I was afraid I might not get to see him again!

He greeted me by rubbing against my leg, then he jumped onto the arm of the sofa and settled in under the warm reading lamp. I petted him, and he purred, and I blinked at him, and he blinked back.

We also bought him a get-well present: a small plastic fountain with a pump so he can always have fresh running water.

I called Maybelle and told her Taco was better. She sounded happy for me.

Weird that one month ago, I hadn't even met Taco, and now I sometimes get sad or happy or scared because of him.

Weird that one month ago, I hadn't really noticed Zara, and now she affects my moods too.

I've been thinking: Zara is not a terrible person. And it's not terrible that she is *outspoken* (just like it's not terrible that Pip is *soft-spoken*). It is, however, hard to get used to Maybelle having a close friend besides me. But maybe there's enough of Maybelle to go around?

AVA, ATTEMPTING TO BE ACCEPTING

P.S. Since Zara messed things up with Chuck, it's not like I'm 100 percent accepting either.

1/18
BEDTIME

Dear Diary,

Pip kept pressuring me to write the Y and Z poems. I didn't feel like it, and it's only Monday. But Pip wouldn't stop asking, so I finally wrote them. Here they are:

Y is for yellowtail.

The pretty yellowtail swims with speed and grace;
If you ran and it swam, it would be a close race.

Z is for zebrafish.

Zebrafish have stripes that are shiny and blue;
A zeal of zebras are black, white, and furry too.

I hope Jerry Valentino likes our book even though, as Dad might say, it finishes with a whimper and not a bang.

Frankly, I'm glad the English alphabet has only twenty-six letters. Pip says the Spanish alphabet is longer because of *ñ* (as in *mañana*) and *ll* (as in *llama*) and *rr* (as in *guitarra*) and *ch* (as in *mucho*). Mrs. Lemons once said that the Japanese language has *three* different alphabets.

Anyway, my part is done. Z is for zebrafish and now Z is for zzzzzs.

I wish Taco would sleep with me instead of going prowling around at night.

At least he's back home. Tonight he rolled onto his back asking for a tummy rub, so I rubbed his tummy. Fifteen seconds later, he wriggled upright as if to say, "How dare you rub my tummy?"

He definitely has a mind of his own!

Just now, I took a bath and the door creaked open. I thought it was Pip or Mom or Dad and was about to yell, "Don't come in!" but it was Taco! He put his paws on the rim of the tub and stared at me. I went to pet him, but my hand was dripping wet, so he ran away.

Ava in a Towel

P.S. Tonight's Meatless Monday was bulgur wheat and pea pods. Worst yet!!!

1/19
BEFORE SCHOOL

DEAR DIARY,

Last night, I was almost asleep when I heard a sound in my room. What was it? Could it be? Yes! It was…Taco!! He came padding over and jumped right up onto my bed. I could hardly believe it!

At first, he stayed near my feet. I didn't want to scare him away, so I stayed stock-still. Then I drummed my fingers to invite him to come a little closer.

He crept up and stopped just above my knee where I could pet him. He was almost out of reach, but I stretched out my arm and brushed his fur with my fingertips. He crept a smidge closer and stayed there for a few minutes. I thought he might let me curl up with him, but he turned around and faced my feet—in case he wanted to make a speedy getaway.

Which he did, right as I was about to drift off.

At breakfast, I told everyone that Taco had come to visit me. I was afraid Pip or Dad or Mom would say, "He sleeps with me every night," or "I was wondering where he went." But they didn't. Mom said, "One night in a vet's cage, the next in a bedroom. He's no fool." Dad quoted Charles Dickens who said, "What greater gift than the love of a cat." And Pip just said, "You're lucky." I admitted that Taco stayed for only a few minutes, and by my knee, not in my arms. Pip said, "You're still lucky."

I know I am. Taco is a good cat—and maybe he finally realizes that I'm a good kid.

AVA, LUCKY

P.S. I have to hurry and get ready for school! Funny that today in the world, I'll see lots of people, but the only people Taco will see are us. We *are* his world.

1/19
RIGHT AFTER SCHOOL (USING MY TIGER PEN)

DEAR DIARY,

I decided I should try harder to talk to Chuck, so I asked if he finished the book. He looked confused. I added, "The boxer one. The one you got at the bookstore."

"Oh right," he said. "Yes, it was good." He asked if I'd been using the tiger pen I'd bought. Well, that broke the ice, and I said, "Yes," and then we both looked right at each other and smiled for, like, two seconds. Maybe even three.

I was glad that just as a bad question can mess things up, a good question can fix things up. Or start to, anyway.

"You'll appreciate this, Ava," Chuck said, opening his spelling notebook and digging out the test from last Friday. "I got a 75—but I got one of the bonus words right: 'illiterate.' So I'm *not* illiterate! I can read and write!"

I laughed.

"Is your 100s streak still going strong?" he asked.

"It is," I said, and might have blushed a little. *Do* I like Chuck a teeny bit? Or am I just relieved that we're friends again?

He showed me two words that he got wrong. He'd spelled

"sophomore" "soft more" and he spelled "self-esteem" "self a steam." I laughed, and the good thing was that he knew that I was laughing *with* him, not *at* him.

Ava, Smiling

1/22
Friday After School

Dear Diary,

I was starving, so after school, I heated up some alphabet soup. I love alphabet soup. I always spoon out one A and eat it first.

In school, when it was time to grade our spelling tests, we had to pick a partner. Chuck and I looked right at each other at the exact same time and switched papers without even saying anything. He got another 75 and I got another 100.

One of the words he got wrong was "caterpillar." In front of the whole class, he asked Mrs. Lemons, "What are caterpillars afraid of?" She hesitated, so he answered "*Dog*erpillars!"

Mrs. Lemons laughed. The funny thing is that our math teacher, Miss Hamshire, never thinks Chuck is funny. She thinks Maybelle can do no wrong and Chuck can do no right.

In the library, Pip and I gave our book to Mr. Ramirez to give to Jerry Valentino. I hope he can help us get it published!

I wonder if Jerry Valentino has already started reading *Alphabet Fish*. If so, I wonder what letter he is up to?

ABC Ava with Hopes and Dreams

1/24
4:21

Dear Diary,

It's still light outside because the sun is staying out longer now than it did last month. I like long summer days more than short winter ones. Maybe everyone does?

Dad made us all little Sunday sundaes. Even Taco was hanging out in the kitchen.

Mom gave Taco his last dose of medicine (she's way better at squirting it into his mouth than Dad is). Then she started taking photos of him.

Dad said, "The cat as *muse*!"

"Taco *mews*!" I said, as if we were playing the Homonym Game.

"You guys are a-*mus*-ing!" Pip chimed.

Taco pushed his forehead against my shin as if asking to be petted in return for all his posing. Mom took more photos, including one of Dad and Pip and me, and then stretched out her hand and took one of all four of us. It was not a selfie; it was a family-ie.

Question: Has Taco made us more of a family??

Ava, Musing and Amusing

P.S. I think having Taco *has* helped us all be in a good mood. (Except on weekend mornings when Mom and Dad say he wakes them too early.)

1/25
AFTER DINNER

DEAR DIARY,

In the library today, Mr. Ramirez handed me an envelope from Jerry Valentino. I have to confess: when I opened it, I was expecting something very different.

Mr. Ramirez could tell from my expression that Jerry Valentino didn't think our book was about to take the world by storm.

I'm going to staple the letter in here, even if it means I have to cut it in two. (Note: I might enjoy cutting it in two!)

Dear Ava Wren,

I was glad for the opportunity to take a look at *Alphabet Fish*, particularly because I remember meeting you at Misty Oaks Library last October and reading your unusual story about the queen bee. I am pleased to see that you are still writing and that you and your sister have been able to work together. It is clear that you both have talent and have gone to considerable effort. I applaud you for that.

If Mr. Ramirez had asked for just a quick reaction, I might have said, "Bravo!" and "Well done!" and that would be that.

But since Mr. Ramirez asked me about "the possibility of publication," I feel I should let you know that the marketplace for picture books is very tight, and most editors are not keen on rhyming books. *The Cat in the Hat* aside, successful rhymes are deceptively difficult. There's also the question of the audience for *Alphabet Fish*. Do most children care about mudskippers or queen triggerfish? Can they relate? (A stickler might question whether a jellyfish is a fish at all.)

I'm looking forward to working with your grade next Tuesday and Friday, and we will talk more about writing then. For now, Ava, think about what inspires *you*. Is it fish? Or might there be another subject closer to your heart? And can you come up with a real story someday, one with a beginning, middle, and end? Is there something you are ardent about?

I hope you don't find my candor discouraging. I like the way you use words, and I admire your ambition.

Respectfully yours,

Jerry Valentino

I showed the letter to Mr. Ramirez. "Aren't I too young to get a rejection letter?" I asked.

"He's an author, not an editor, so technically, it's not a rejection letter," he said, reading it. "And it's very respectful, even though, okay, he doesn't think you hit a home run your first time at bat." (Mr. Ramirez was using a baseball metaphor.) "Look, maybe he should be taking *me* to task for putting thoughts into your young heads."

"Pip *was* excited," I confessed. "And his 'candor' *is* 'discouraging.'"

"Can you break it to her gently?" Mr. Ramirez said. "Or do you want me to?"

"I will."

At home, I showed Dad the letter. He was making *ratatouille*, which is a hard spelling word as well as a gross vegetarian dish. Dad read the letter all the way through. "Publication at this stage probably wasn't a very realistic expectation," he said, putting his hand on my shoulder. "But hard work is its own reward. And you and Pip had fun doing it, right?"

"Most of the time," I said and made a face.

Dad smiled because he knows that Pip and I don't allllllways get along any more than he and Uncle Patrick allllllways got along. "You're talented, Ava," he said. "And you're disciplined. If you want to write a book or a play someday, I have no doubt you'll do it."

"I don't want to write a play," I said, because Dad's the playwright, not me. I almost added, "But I *do* want to write a book." I didn't though, because I'm not ready to say that out loud, not even to Dad.

"Want to slice veggies with me?" Dad asked.

"Sure," I said, and he showed me how small he wanted the pieces. I swear, sometimes it seems as if Meatless Mondays come way more than once a week!

We chopped and chopped, and when I cut into an onion, my eyes got teary, and I pretended it was because of the rejection letter.

Dad knew I was kidding, but when Pip came home, I showed her the letter, and it was obvious that she really was disappointed. She tried to hide it, but at dinner she was almost as quiet as she used to be. When I think about it, Pip *had* spent way more time on the fish drawings than I had on the rhymes.

Just now, we were brushing our teeth, and Pip said, "I wish he'd liked it."

At first I said, "What?" (Actually, I said, "Whaaa?" because my mouth was full of toothpaste.) But then I said, "Me too."

"And I wish we could reject his rejection letter," she added.

I nodded and spat and said that at least Jerry Valentino hadn't said anything bad about her illustrations, just about my words. Which was true, but also nice and unselfish of me to point out.

Ava, Altruistic (that means nice and unselfish)

1/25
IN BED

DEAR DIARY,

Pip knocked on my door and said, "I might make a flower alphabet book called *Z is for Zinnia*. It could be all pictures, no rhymes."

"Great idea!" I said because I didn't want her to ask me to write twenty-six flower rhymes.

Truth is, I think Pip likes working by herself as much as she likes collaborating. In school, I often like working by myself more than doing "teamwork" or "group work" too. (Exception: I like when Chuck and I switch spelling tests.)

Anyway, I just read an Aesop fable, and it was so scary that I feel like knocking on Mom and Dad's door. But I haven't done that in a long time.

The story is called "The One-Eyed Doe" and goes like this:

A deer that had lost an eye was grazing on a high cliff near the sea. She liked grazing there because she could keep her good eye toward the land and be on the lookout for hunters, and keep her blind eye toward the sea where she assumed she was safe. One day, however, a sailor on a ship noticed how beautiful she was and took his bow and arrow and shot her dead. As she drew her last breath, she realized (and this is the moral): "Trouble can come from where you least expect it."

After reading that unhappy ending, I did *not* want to turn my light off, so I reread Jerry Valentino's letter one more time, and it got me thinking: What subjects *are* close to my heart? What *am* I "ardent" about? ("Ardent" is when you care a lot about something.)

Ava, Ardent

1/26
FIRST THING IN THE MORNING

Dear Diary,

Did Taco sense that I'd gotten bad news and read a bad fable? Last night he jumped onto my bed and instead of staying by my feet or knees, he nestled right up in the crook of my arm. He didn't *face* my *face*, but he waved his tail once so that the soft white tip brushed the bottom of my chin. It tickled and was so sweet. I didn't think cats could do that.

Then he did something even sweeter: he purred! In the dark with me!

It was the first time he'd ever purred in my bed, and it made me happy—especially since that bummer letter had bummed me out and that creepy fable had given me the creeps! Everything was silent in my room except for Taco's *rumble bumble rumble bumble*. It sounded louder than ever, but also warm and comforting and peaceful and...hypnotizing.

For the first time, he also pressed his paws against my side, first one then the other, one then the other. It was like he was giving me a *massage* and a *message*. Was he saying, "I love you"?

Mom once told me that what some people call "kneading," others call "making biscuits."

Then, all of a sudden, for absolutely no reason, Taco stopped and ran off.

That's how he rolls.

Still, it was nice while it lasted!

Pip likes to go to sleep with a book, but me, I'd rather go to sleep with a cat.

Ava, About to Be Late to School

1/26
BEDTIME

Dear Diary,

I don't know how much I can write tonight because we wrote a ton in school today, and there's only so much writing a *hand* can...*hand*le!

Besides, I'm not Ava the Ambidextrous—I'm Ava the Rightie. If I were ambidextrous, maybe I could switch hands whenever my writing hand got tired. (Then again, brains get tired too.)

So here's what happened:

Jerry Valentino came to our classroom. He's as tall and skinny as ever, but his straggly hair is longer than it was in October, and this time he wore it in a ponytail. I bet Principal Gupta was shocked that our school's special guest had a ponytail, but I guess there's no dress code for grown-ups.

Anyway, Mrs. Lemons introduced Jerry Valentino and lifted up our class copy of *Campfire Nights*. It had been read, reread, and *re*reread so many times that someone should have ordered a new one by now. The book is missing a corner of its cover!

Well, I was worried that Jerry Valentino might say out loud what he'd said in his letter (that my rhymes were lame and who cares about fish?). But he didn't. He just looked out at us all, including Maybelle, Zara, Chuck, Riley, and the three Emilys, and said he wanted to help us become better writers. He talked about his six best writing tips and we copied them down. Here they are:

CREATIVE WRITING TIPS

1. Write from the heart: write about what you care about.
2. Use your head: think about beginning, middle, and end.
3. Show, don't just tell: it's better to reveal than to explain.
4. Use your senses: sight, smell, sound, taste, touch.
5. Provide details: paint pictures with words.
6. Read your work aloud: listen to the rhythm and music of the words.

Next he said he was going to give us a "prompt."

"What's a prompt?" Riley asked.

Jerry Valentino said it was a word or phrase that he hoped would "spark ideas" and inspire us. He said we would write for five minutes, and afterward, we'd go around the room and share our work aloud, and everyone would say something positive.

"Only positive?" Zara asked.

"Only positive," Jerry Valentino said.

"You mean we can't hold our noses and say, 'P.U. That stinks!'?" Chuck joked.

"Chuck, please." Mrs. Lemons scowled at him. Chuck gave me a tiny smile, so I gave him a tiny smile back.

Jerry Valentino said, "Is everyone ready?"

Amir said, "Should we use lined paper?"

Mrs. Lemons said yes.

Zara said, "Can I sharpen my pencil?"

Mrs. Lemons said, "Make it quick."

Emily Jenkins said, "Can I go to the bathroom?"

Mrs. Lemons looked exasperated. "Can't you wait five minutes?"

Finally, Jerry Valentino gave us the first prompt. It was: "my grandfather's hands."

At first, everyone looked confused, but then everyone (except me) wrote and wrote and wrote until he said to stop.

Soon everyone shared their writing out loud, and he didn't let anyone apologize ahead of time even though Emily Sherman started to say she didn't get to finish.

He said she could finish at home if she wanted and not to worry because what we were doing was more like "sketching with words" than "creating polished prose."

Well, Chuck was the first to read out loud. He wrote about how his grandfather taught him to box with big brown soft gloves. I said, "That was really good" because it was.

Zara wrote that her grandfather's hands are rough and calloused and "have dirt under the fingernails." Riley said, "Dirt is a good detail."

Emily LaCasse wrote about how her grandfather used to play the piano, but now his hands have spots on them and one pinkie bends the wrong way. Jerry Valentino said, "Nice!" which was weird because it was *not* nice that his pinkie bends the wrong way and is funny-looking, but I guess Jerry Valentino meant that he liked the detail.

Maybelle wrote about how her grandfather was "a card shark" whose hands always "held an ace." Jerry Valentino said her writing was "very clever."

I wrote just one sentence saying that I'd never gotten to meet either of my grandfathers and that this was a shame. Chuck said that was sad. But Jerry Valentino said I should have asked for a different prompt.

That made me mad because how was I supposed to know? Everyone had been scribbling away, and the classroom was so pin-drop quiet that I thought I was doing the right thing by not interrupting.

Fortunately, he gave us a brand-new prompt. He said to write about something "warm and comforting."

Everyone started writing a mile a minute, including me.

Later, we went around the room again. Emily Sherman wrote about hot chicken soup after a snowball fight. Emily LaCasse wrote about how her baby blanket had been washed so many times it was "the size of a dish rag." Emily Jenkins wrote about the "gentle sound of summer rain" on the roof of her camp cabin. Riley wrote about her pony's sweaty neck. Maybelle wrote about the gingerbread her great aunt used to make, back when Maybelle used to help push her around in a wheelchair. And Chuck wrote about his stuffed animal, Buffalo Billy, and how he used to sleep with it when he was little, but it always ended up on the floor, and then he'd feel bad, so now Buffalo Billy sits on a shelf. Chuck seemed embarrassed after reading that aloud, but I said it was sweet.

Mostly everyone said good things about everyone else's words, and I think the exercise helped us all get to know each other better—even though most of us (besides Zara) had already known each other for years.

Guess what I wrote about?

Correct! Taco Cat and his warm and comforting rumbly bumbly purring!

Jerry Valentino said we'd all done "fine work" and if anyone wanted to take the prompt home and develop it into a longer story, he'd be happy to take a look on Friday. I think most people (like Chuck and Jamal) thought, "No way," because this was extra credit, not homework. But I was thinking, "Way!"

I also felt a little shift happening inside me. Or maybe a big one?

It was like, deep inside my body, for three or four seconds, everything went totally still because I was making a decision. No, I was making a *plan*. No, I was making a…*commitment*! (That's a bonus word that's like a promise.)

In his letter, Jerry Valentino had asked if there might be another subject closer to my heart. Obviously, my cat is closer to my heart than angelfish, bumblebee fish, or *cat*fish—combined. (For a while, maybe Taco really *was* my "primary topic of conversation.")

My hand shot up into the air. "Can I try to turn what I wrote into a children's book?"

"*May* I, not *can* I," he corrected. "And sure, you may."

I wanted to say, "I'm glad I *may* and I hope I *can*!" But I didn't. Besides, my brain was already busy thinking about the story I wanted to write. It kept coming up with ideas and I kept taking notes.

Now I'm yawning and yawning, so I am calling it a night.

Ambitious Ava, Inspired but Tired

P.S. Should I ask Pip to draw a cover for the new book? I don't think so. She might be better at fish and flowers than cats and people anyway.

1/28
BEDTIME

DEAR DIARY,

I didn't write in you yesterday because I'd already spent a zillion hours writing and rewriting a picture book I'm calling "The Cat Who Wouldn't Purr." I tried to use my heart and my head, to show not just tell, to use senses and details, and to think about the rhythm and music of words.

I also employed alliteration and onomatopoeia and poetic license. And I made Pip a character (sort of). I even read my work aloud before pressing print, which Dad says real writers do.

It was not easy. It was work. But it was fun work (which seems like an oxymoron but might not be).

What I mean is: I liked feeling so focused. Instead of my mind being in lots of places, it was in just one place. And I was in charge. In real life, I don't have that much control over my cat or my friends or my family, but I guess I do have control over my work, or at least what words I put on what page.

Like, you can't 100 percent count on other people, but if you do your best, maybe you can count on yourself.

Last year, Mrs. (Bright) White said that if you have talent, you "owe it to yourself and others to put it to good use."

Well, I tried anyway.

I am now stapling one copy here, and tomorrow I will give a copy to Jerry Valentino. I hope he likes it more than *Alphabet Fish*. I revised this story so many times, I don't know if this is the fifteenth draft—or *fiftieth*. I kept thinking, "Ta-da! I'm done!" but then I kept making changes.

And now, without further ado, ta-da! Here's:

The Cat Who Wouldn't Purr

by Ava Wren, Age Eleven

Once upon a time, two sisters brought home a cat.
At first, the cat was very shy and very scared.
For three days, he hid in the dark under the sofa.
On day four, he crept out, whiskers first.

He found many things he liked to do.

He liked to nibble the tops of tulips.
He liked to drink water from the faucet.
He liked to burrow in brown bags.
And he liked to nap by the fireplace.

But he would not purr.

He liked to smell shoes that came in from outside.
He liked to watch movies on TV.

He liked to chase string and ping-pong balls and laser lights.
And he liked to nap on folded clothes, warm from the dryer.

But he would not purr.

He liked to hunt for flies.
He liked to sprawl on books.
He liked to step on keyboards and type mmmms and zzzzs and jwfqs.
And he liked to nap in a corner of the closet, by the slippers.

But he would not purr.

The two sisters began to feel impatient,
But they tried to keep the faith and
Respect their cat's inner nature.
Because you can't force a cat to do anything—

Especially purr!

One morning, after nibbling and chasing and hunting,
The cat found a rhombus of sunshine on the rug.
He licked himself, yawned, and tucked in his tail.

He put one paw over his eyes and curled up for a catnap.

Did he purr?
No, he did not.

The younger sister began to brush the cat's fur.
She brushed slowly and gently, slowly and gently.
After a while, a long, long, long while,
She heard a funny, soft sound coming from deep inside the cat:

rumble bumble rumble bumble rumble bumble

She motioned for her sister to come over.
The older sister tiptoed over and began to pet the cat.
She pet his fur slowly and gently, slowly and gently.
And she heard the same sound coming from deep inside the cat:

rumble bumble rumble bumble rumble bumble

The two sisters smiled at each other,
The cat stayed in the sunshine and did not scamper off.

He let the girls brush him and pet him.
He even let them put their ears on his soft fur to listen to his

rumble bumble rumble bumble rumble bumble
rumble bumble rumble bumble rumble bumble

And he kept right on purring and purring and purring—
Safe and sound and snug in his brand-new home.

AVA WREN, AUTHOR FOR REAL

1/29
FRIDAY NIGHT

DEAR DIARY,

Today was ridiculously exciting!

Not only was the author Jerry Valentino in our class, but so were both librarians—Mr. Ramirez and Mrs. (Bright) White—as well as a reporter (Rebecca) and a photographer (Rafael) from the *Misty Oaks Monitor*! We were supposed to act like everything was normal, but that was impossible with so many grown-ups around.

I kept watching them watching us and observing them observing us. They were looking at our classroom walls with the stapled-up drawings and handwritten compositions and posters about good habits and how to be a model middle school kid. I wondered what they thought of Mrs. Lemons's poster of a dog with glasses saying, "Bad spelling! Poor grammar! I cannot eat this homework!" And what they thought of our nutrition poster with its pea pods saying, "Peas try me," and cheese saying, "Choose cheese." Did they think it was cheesy?

I also observed the reporter reading the sign on Mrs. Lemons's desk that says, "Teachers touch tomorrow."

Today's first prompt was "playground accident," and we all wrote for five minutes. I wrote about the time I fell off the monkey bars, but I confess, I was distracted because I'd given Jerry Valentino my "manuscript," and while we were writing, he was *reading*!

Soon, we were sharing our playground accident stories out loud. Chuck's was the funniest. His was about when he was in kindergarten and he *had an accident* during recess. He actually peed on the slide because he hadn't realized he'd needed to go to the boys' room!

The second prompt was "frostbite or sunburn." Everyone wrote and wrote, and then we shared our stories. Today's stories were even better than Tuesday's because we've learned new techniques, and as Jerry Valentino put it, we were "digging deeper."

At the end of class, Jerry Valentino asked if I'd mind if he read my picture book out loud. I said no, but to be honest, inside I felt a little shaky. I never imagined that he'd read my words aloud with his deep author voice and with grown-up strangers in the room. But he did. And you know what? I thought my words sounded good. I hoped others thought so too.

"Any comments?" he asked.

Zara was the first to say she liked it, and I saw the photographer, Rafael, take a few pictures.

I looked at Chuck and he gave me a thumbs-up.

Maybelle said she liked "the rhythm of the words."

Riley said she liked the "specific details," and that it reminded her of a cat in her barn who likes to groom himself and how afterward, the tip of his tongue sometimes sticks out. Emily Sherman said, "I liked your story too, and that's saying a lot because I'm a dog person. I have a bichon frisé and a maltipoo. Cats give me hives."

Jerry Valentino jumped in and said he admired my "vivid verbs" and "colorful details" and "suspenseful buildup," and his only suggestion was for me to cut the opening "Once upon a time," because those words were cliché and not needed.

"You can cross them out," I said. He smiled and said, "*May* I?" I said, "Yes. You *may*. Please do. Thank you." He took his pencil and crossed out the four words.

At the end of the workshop, he told us all to be aware of how much "original and evocative" writing we could do in just five minutes. He said that whether we became authors or not, *everybody* writes messages and emails and reports and thank-you notes, so we should always strive to "have something to say and to say it well." He also gave us bonus pointers like "Avoid repetition," adding, "Unless you're repeating specific words or phrases on purpose, as Ava did so effectively."

After class, I didn't want anyone to think I was a teacher's pet, so I started to zoom out the door. But Jerry Valentino asked me to stay for a moment. So I did. Then he asked what inspired me. That was funny because last time he'd asked was in October in the Misty Oaks Library. This time, instead of talking to a big audience, I told my answer just to him, Mrs. Lemons, the reporter, and the photographer.

"Taco Cat!" I said and explained that I'd convinced my

parents to let me rescue a cat, but that, at first, he'd done nothing but hide.

The reporter took notes, and the photographer asked if it would be okay to take a photo of me and my cat.

I was surprised but said, "I guess."

"Are you free today after school?"

"This could be a human interest story for the Sunday paper," Rafael explained and handed me his cell phone. "Do you want to call your parents?"

I looked at Mrs. Lemons, and she was sort of beaming, so I said, "Okay." I was hoping Dad was home and would say, "Sure."

And he was. And he did.

Next thing you know, the reporter, the photographer, and I were in our living room. Taco was mostly keeping his distance while Dad was helping us get ready for the "photo shoot." Dad was moving stacks of newspapers and plumping up cushions while I changed into a red blouse and brushed my hair. When Rafael said he was all set, I picked up Taco and sat on the sofa, and for way over a minute, Taco didn't even wriggle. It was like he was posing too. And even though nobody did my makeup or adjusted lights or said, "Action!" the whole experience made me feel kind of like a movie star. So it was easy to smile for the camera. (When Rafael said, "Say 'Cheese!'" I thought of how, when Chuck takes pictures, he says, "Say 'Boogies!'")

Rebecca called her editor at the *Misty Oaks Monitor*, and said that if the paper had our permission and "enough space," they might want to run not just the photo, but also my cat book and cat haiku.

I said, "Okay," and Dad smiled. It was exciting that everything was happening so fast!

"This will be a feel-good story, if you will," Rebecca added.

"I will," I said, because it was all making *me* feel good.

Pip might never want her picture in the paper. But me, I love attention. The more, the merrier!

AVA WREN DOES IT AGAIN!

1/30
Saturday afternoon

Dear Diary,

The big news today was that Dad made his famous Irish breakfast.

Will the big news tomorrow be me me me? Will *I* wake up famous?

Ava, Anonymous (a bonus word that means when people don't know who you are)

1/31
Sunday Morning

Dear Diary,

Dad woke me with a giant smile on his face and handed me the newspaper. He never hands me the newspaper. He and Mom sometimes hand it to each other, but it's not like I care about town hall meetings or grocery store coupons.

"Take a look," Dad said.

Well, my eyes almost popped out of my head (gross metaphor) because Taco and I were on the front page!!! In color!!! And GIANT!!! There was a big photo of me with my red blouse and Taco with his white zigzag. And we looked pretty cute, if I do say so myself. (I hope that doesn't sound conceited.)

"Whoa, Dad, I had no idea—" I started to read the article about Jerry Valentino, when I saw, right next to it, "The Cat Who Wouldn't Purr"! There they were, my very own words (minus "Once upon a time")!

Our phone, which rarely rings unless there's an emergency or, like, an election, started ringing and ringing. Maybelle called and both her parents got on. Even Mr. Ramirez called! Mom called Nana Ethel, and she said, "Congratulations!" And Dad emailed Uncle Patrick the link to the article, photo, story, and haiku, and he said it was "the cat's pajamas" (which Dad said is a compliment).

And okay, I know the *Misty Oaks Monitor* is not *The New York Times* or whatever, but it is all very exciting!

Bea called too. She said her mom had thumbtacked the article to the bulletin board in Bates Books and scribbled, "a young writer to watch."

"Really?" I asked because last fall, Bea's mom had said I was a "young writer with a lot to learn."

"Really," Bea said. "She even tacked up one of your snowflakes next to it."

"Cool," I said because it *was* cool. So cool!

Ava Wren, Young Writer to Watch

2/1 AFTER DINNER (WHICH WAS COUSCOUS WITH BOK CHOY AND SUN-DRIED TOMATOES)

DEAR DIARY,

The newspaper article was posted on the bulletin board outside Principal Gupta's office with two thumbtacks, one yellow, one green. A lot of people, from the nurse to the custodian to the lunch lady, said nice things to me. Even scary Miss Hamshire, with her googly glasses. And even Alex Gladstone, the fourth-grader who got first prize in last year's library contest for his story about Ernie the Earthworm.

Monday scrambled is *dynamo*, and I guess today was very dynamic.

It was fun to have so many people come up to me. Embarrassing too—but mostly fun.

Chuck said, "I can't believe I have a famous friend! I thought you had to rob a bank to get your picture in the paper!" He told me two jokes, one about spelling and one about cats.

Joke One:

Question: Why is Old MacDonald a bad speller?

Answer: Because he adds E I E I O to every word.

Joke Two:

Question: When is it bad luck to see a black cat?

Answer: When you're a mouse.

Both jokes made me L-O-L—but Chuck can make me laugh just by flapping his arm and making farty noises. (Which is *sophomoric*, I know.)

Anyway, all this attention made me remember a story I wrote before vacation. It was called "Invisible Girl," and Dad and Mrs. Lemons had both liked it. "Invisible Girl" was about a girl who could disappear at will. At first, she thinks it's a fun trick. Then she gets lonely and realizes she'd much rather be visible than invisible.

Ava Wren, the Opposite of Invisible

2/1
IN BED

DEAR DIARY,

Tonight Mom put beets in the salad. I don't usually like colorful things in my salad; I like my salad green. But the beets were surprisingly okay. I even tried a brussels sprout. It was *bitter*, but *better* than I thought.

At dinner, Mom said Dr. Gross's entire staff got a kick out of seeing Taco in the paper. "And seeing *you* too!" she added. "Bob, we should frame the newspaper story, don't you think?"

Dad said, "Absolutely." (They've already framed three of Pip's drawings. Not that I've counted.)

After dinner, the phone rang and I picked up. A lady named Gretchen said she'd read the article and wanted to "drop by." She said she lived in Vernon Valley, which is "twenty minutes to the north." She sounded nervous, which was weird, but said that if tomorrow at 4:30 worked for me, it worked for her.

"Will one of your parents be there?" she asked.

"Probably my dad," I said.

After we hung up, a tiny part of me wondered if she was a scout for *The Today Show*. Or if she ran a publishing company and needed a book about cats. Maybe a happy book about a girl and her cat.

I mean, there are plenty of books out there about a boy and his dog. Pip went through a pile of them. *Old Yeller* and *Where the Red Fern Grows* and *The Call of the Wild* and *Beautiful Joe*. Most had unhappy endings, and when Pip would turn the last page, she'd be in a puddle on the sofa.

Pip galloped through horse books too, like *Black Beauty* and *National Velvet* and *The Red Pony* and *Misty of Chincoteague*. And *Seabiscuit*, which is for grown-ups. They had sad or scary parts too.

Anyway, there was something strange in the lady's tone. Why had she sounded nervous when *she's* the grown-up? Kids get nervous talking to grown-ups, not the other way around. And why had I told her she could come over? What if she's a...kidnapper??

I guess I could have mentioned this to Mom or Dad, but so many people called that I forgot.

AVA, A LITTLE APPREHENSIVE (WHICH MEANS WORRIED)

2/2 Groundhog Day (Well, Groundhog Night)

Dear Diary,

I've never had a day like this and I never want to again!!

At school this morning, I mentioned to Maybelle that a stranger was dropping by and that she had sounded nervous on the phone. Maybelle offered to come over, but said she was supposed to hang out with Zara, so could they both come? I said sure. And for once, I didn't even mind.

At 4:30 sharp, the doorbell rang. Mom was at work, Dad was running errands, and Pip, Maybelle, Zara, and I were in the living room. I peeked through the keyhole and saw a tall, skinny woman with short, fluffy, white hair standing in a red coat. She looked basically normal, so I opened the door.

I wish I hadn't!!!

She said she was Gretchen Guthrie and started complimenting my "nice story" about the "nice cat." I said thank you and noticed she kept looking all around. Suddenly Taco came bounding down the stairs, his white-tipped tail high in the air. He rubbed his zigzag against her shin and began weaving in and out of her legs.

"This is Taco," I said. I didn't get why Taco was being so friendly. Did the lady have catnip in her pockets?

She stooped down to pet him.

"May I pick him up?"

"He doesn't like being picked up," I said, but she scooped him up anyway and held him close and breathed him in. And Taco didn't mind! He didn't wriggle away or bite her nose or scratch her cheek or anything.

"What a cat," she said, and her voice caught. Pip and Maybelle and Zara stood up and walked over.

"This is my sister, Pip," I said. "And these are my friends, Maybelle and Zara." The word "friends" popped right out, which Zara probably appreciated.

Gretchen introduced herself while still holding on to Taco. Pip leaned in and scratched Taco behind the ears and under his chin.

"He likes that," the lady said, which was odd. Then she asked, "Are your parents here?"

"Our dad will be back soon," Pip replied. "He's buying groceries." I'd totally forgotten to tell Dad that she was coming by.

"I'll come back." She gave Taco a kiss on his head, which bothered me (though it didn't bother Taco), and put him down.

She left, and I shut the door behind her, glad it was just us kids again.

"She's a little weird," Zara pronounced. "Don't you think?"

None of us said anything, but none of us disagreed.

Zara marched to the living room window and pulled back the

curtain. "She got back into her car, but she's just sitting there," she reported. "I changed my mind: she's not *a little* weird; she's *a lot* weird."

"*Dangerous* weird?" Pip asked. "Like, Stranger Danger, let's call nine-one-one, weird?"

"I don't think so," I answered. "She was sweet to Taco."

"Too sweet," Zara pronounced. "All snuggly-wuggly." (Note: Zara wasn't bugging me as much as usual, probably because I was agreeing with what she was saying.) "Why isn't she leaving?" she asked. "Does she have a flat tire? Is she out of gas?"

"Is her battery dead?" Pip added.

"Is *she* dead?" Zara said.

Maybelle joined Zara by the window. After a minute, Maybelle said, "Hey, Ava, your dad just pulled into the driveway."

When Dad walked in with a bag of groceries, Zara announced, "Mr. Wren, a lady came while you were gone, and she's just sitting in her car out front, across the street. She hasn't left."

"A lady?" Dad said.

Zara pointed out the window and said, "A lady who looks like a Q-tip." Now all five of us were peeking out at Gretchen. She must have seen us because she got out of her car and came walking toward our door.

"Who is she?" Dad asked, still holding the groceries.

"You know how people kept calling yesterday?" I said. "I forgot to tell you that—"

The doorbell rang.

"Do we have to let her back in?" Zara asked. "I have a bad

feeling." Zara grabbed Taco and handed him to Maybelle. Taco started squirming, but Zara said, "Maybelle, take him to Ava's room. Go! Now! NOW!"

Maybelle looked confused, but she slung Taco over her shoulder and ran upstairs, two steps at a time, following orders. Dad looked confused too, but he put down his groceries and opened the door.

A gust of wintery air blew in, and so did Q-tip Lady. She introduced herself, and Dad said, "What can we do for you?"

She said, "Hello, Mr. Wren. I'm afraid we have a situation."

"A situation?" Dad repeated.

"I'm afraid you have my cat."

I swear, I thought I was going to faint on the floor right then and there! Pip and I stared at each other, and Zara started giving the lady the evil eye.

"My sister brought me a copy of the *Monitor* because she recognized Amber on the front page. She knew my cat had gotten lost over Christmas, and that I'd posted photos on Facebook and put flyers in stores. She knew I was *beside* myself! Well, my sister recognized Amber's coloring and his little lightning rod"—she touched her own forehead—"and when she read your daughter's story, she had no doubt." She turned to me, maybe expecting me to say something. But I just stood there in total, utter shock.

"Amber was standoffish with me at first too," she continued. "He's not a natural nuzzler. But you're right. He does like to be brushed, and he likes TV." She smiled at me.

I did not smile back. It was like I'd died inside. I was hoping Dad would ask Gretchen to do an about-face and march out the door. And what was in her hand? Was it a… cat carrier??

"I'm sorry to upset you," she concluded, "but Amber is mine. He belongs to me." She was looking all around for him, expecting him to race over again. "I adopted him four years ago last November, shortly after my husband died. He was just a kitten. Well, last month, my niece came to cat-sit over the holidays, and I guess she left a window open—"

"If you're talking about the cat who was just here," Zara interrupted, "he's dead. It just happened. It's terrible. It's…tragic. We're all, um, *beside* ourselves."

I wondered if Zara had gone nuts, but apparently she was just getting warmed up. "I'm sorry to, um, upset you, but he jumped out another window. I guess he likes windows—*liked*. Only this time he didn't land on his feet, the way cats are supposed to. He landed on his…head, and he died. He's…dead."

I thought for sure Dad was going to say something, but maybe he got distracted by Zara's "improv" skills. (Dad says every actor needs improvisational skills.)

"He's dead," Zara repeated. "*Deceased*. So it doesn't even matter whose cat he was."

Dad put his hand up to shoosh Zara and turned to the lady. "Mrs. Guthrie," he began—but then we all heard a loud strange pounding from above. *Thump. Thump thump! Thump THUMP THUMP!* At first I didn't know what it was. Then I realized it was Taco hurling himself against my bedroom door! He wanted out—probably because he sensed that his "owners" were both downstairs. Gretchen looked up toward the noise, and Taco started yowling and howling. I heard my door open, and we all watched as Taco came flying downstairs.

"Oh, my mistake," Zara mumbled. "I guess he survived." She took a small step back.

"Amber!" Gretchen said. She picked him up and threw him over her shoulder like a scarf.

Taco didn't resist, but he shot me a glance, and I wondered what he was thinking.

"His name isn't Amber," Pip piped up bravely. "It's Taco."

"Taco Cat," I heard myself say. "T-A-C-O-C-A-T. It's a palindrome. Like Ava, A-V-A. And Pip, P-I-P." I gestured toward Dad. "And D-A-D, or, well, B-O-B."

Gretchen nodded. "I'm sorry, Ava." She was looking right at me. "Really, I am."

"I'm sorry too," Maybelle whispered to Zara and me. "I couldn't hold on to him. He was going crazy. He even scratched me a little, though I know he didn't mean it."

"I want to thank all of you very much," Gretchen said, "but now I am going to go ahead and take Amber home. My niece has been feeling terrible. She's going to be so relieved—"

"You can't just *take* him!" Zara practically shouted.

"Mrs. Guthrie," Dad said very calmly, "we adopted this cat on New Year's Eve from the Misty Oaks Rescue Center. We rescued him and he is ours."

"Yes, but I rescued him first," she said. "I got Amber at the ASPCA. I have papers. He was my cat. He was my *kitten*!"

I tried to picture Taco as a playful kitty with matching ears.

"I don't doubt that," Dad replied matter-of-factly. "And clearly Taco is comfortable with you. But we have papers too."

"That's right," Pip said softly.

"I'm sorry," Dad added.

I was grateful to Dad and Pip and even Zara and Maybelle, because mostly I was trying not to faint. Was this really happening? My insides were cramping up.

Gretchen said, "May I sit down?" and sat in Dad's big brown chair before Dad even said "Sure." Her whole body seemed to crumple into it.

Taco (Amber?) rubbed against her legs and jumped onto her lap. He was facing her, and she was stroking him, and watching them gave me a lump in my throat *and* a knot in my stomach. I couldn't believe everything was going so wrong so fast.

"I have years of photos right here on my cell phone." Gretchen started fumbling with her phone to prove it, then realized we weren't doubting her. "And I'm very grateful to you all for taking care of him. Really. I can see he had a rough time." She was rubbing his left ear and examining the jagged part. Taco/Amber was not even objecting.

"Our mom works for a vet," I said, speaking up at last. "He's the one who stitched Taco up. Last week, Taco had another emergency—he couldn't pee—and Dr. Gross took care of him again. And it was on a *Sunday*!" I wanted her to know that we got VIP treatment for his UTI, and we were an excellent... *foster* family?

Gretchen gave me a sad smile, stood up with Taco/Amber, and started heading toward the front door. "I'll just put him in the cat carrier," she said. "And I'll reimburse you for the veterinary expenses. I know how expensive that can be."

I didn't know whether to cry or run to my room. It didn't help that I knew we were both right: Taco was mine...but Amber was hers. I mean, I could say that Gretchen reminded me of Cruella de Vil, but she wasn't really a monster. She was a lonely widow whose cat got lost. And she loved Amber. But *I* loved Taco!!!

Gretchen started lowering Taco/Amber into her cat carrier, and again said that she was "going to take him home."

Dad and I looked at each other. Zara took a step forward and said, "Over our dead bodies!"

Dad said, "Zara, that's enough."

Zara shouted, "It's *not* enough!" and placed herself between Gretchen and our front door. For a second, I thought Zara was going to challenge Gretchen to a duel or something.

Dad ignored Zara, but then he said, "Mrs. Guthrie, you cannot just come into our home and take our cat. He was Ava's birthday present—and he's our family's first pet."

"Not counting Goldy Lox," Pip said, and I nodded.

Dad continued and said very clearly, "So I'm afraid *that* is the 'situation.' The cat belongs to us now." We all watched as Gretchen tried to stuff Taco/Amber into her cat carrier, but he wouldn't go in. He kept sticking out his nose and paws. Soon Gretchen was seeming less sure of herself. Dad softened a little and said, "If you would like to visit him from time to time, you're welcome to."

"Joint custody?!" Zara muttered.

Dad gave Zara a stern look and turned back to Gretchen, "Perhaps you could take care of him when we go on vacation…"

"We never go on vacation," I said. It just slipped out.

Taco/Amber started meowing and was shoving out his paws more and more frantically, and finally Gretchen unzipped the zipper, and he jumped out and raced off. But he came right back and started weaving between her legs *and* my legs. I was glad she didn't try to pick him up again. I didn't either.

"I need some air," Gretchen said, leaning against the wall. Maybe *she* was trying not to faint too. "But this matter has not been settled," she added.

"Yes, it has!" Zara said.

"Zara, be quiet!" Dad scolded. He doesn't usually criticize kids unless he's tutoring them (and that doesn't count because parents *pay* him to be critical).

Gretchen kneeled down to pet Taco/Amber and said, "I'm glad you found such a good family when you needed one." She looked at Dad, then Pip, then me, then back at her cat. "I was so very worried about you," she whispered. "I really, really missed you." She sort of buried her face in his fur, as if she wanted to remember how he smelled.

Well, that got me feeling bad for *her*. Her eyes were all shiny, and she looked as if she might have a breakdown right in our living room, which I hoped she wouldn't.

After that, she didn't say another word. She just gave Amber/ Taco a giant last squeeze and left our house really fast. The door clicked behind her.

"Wow," said Dad.

"Can you believe the nerve of some people?" Zara said.

"I know!" Pip agreed.

"That was crazy!" Maybelle said.

"She's crazy!" Zara said.

I looked at Taco and took a breath. "I don't know," I began. "If I went on vacation, and my niece was supposed to feed my cat, but instead she opened a window, and the cat got out, and someone *adopted* him and renamed him…I'd be upset too."

Zara shrugged. "Finders keepers, losers weepers!"

"She *did* seem like she was about to weep," Pip said.

"She did," Maybelle agreed.

"Kids, Taco is *our* cat," Dad said. "We didn't make anything up."

"But she didn't make anything up either," I said. "And it wasn't her fault that her husband died, and her niece was a bad cat-sitter, and her cat jumped out the window. Cats are naturally curious."

"It *was* her fault she named him Amber," Zara said. "She should never have done that to a boy cat!"

"It *is* a terrible name for a boy cat," Maybelle agreed.

"She could have named him Leo or Lightning or Simba or *anything* else," Zara stated.

"Lightning would have been good," Pip agreed.

"On a scale of one to ten of boy cat names," Zara said, "Amber is a two and Taco Cat is a ten."

"Exactly," Maybelle said.

Zara walked back to her spying spot. "I swear, something is seriously *wrong* with that lady! She still hasn't left! She's just sitting in her car, leaning her head on the steering wheel." Zara shook her head. "Go away!" she said into the darkness. "Why are you still here?"

I walked toward the window. "There's nothing *wrong* with her," I said. "She doesn't want to leave without her cat. I can't blame her for that. She *loves* him!"

"Ava," Pip said, "it's not *her* cat. It's *your* cat."

"He was hers first and for much longer," I said, looking at Amber/Taco, who was now pacing by the front door even though he'd never before asked to be let out. He even meowed once. "He was hers first, fair and square. For four *years*."

"And now he's *yours*, fair and square," Zara said. "He probably ran away on purpose!"

"I don't think so," I said quietly. "And it doesn't feel one hundred percent right for us to keep Amber."

"It's *not* Amber. It's Taco!" Dad said. "And, sweetie, things hardly ever feel one hundred percent right."

"I know but…" I picked up Amber/Taco, and slung him over my shoulder and tried to wear him like a scarf, but he wouldn't let me. So I held him in my arms, the regular way. "Is she still out there?"

"Yes," Zara said. "She obviously has a screw loose!"

Well, maybe *I* had a screw loose, because next thing you know, I opened the front door, holding tight to Amber/Taco.

I went down our front walk, looking both ways because Mom and Dad always say, "Better a second of your life than your life in a second." I crossed the street and approached Gretchen's car and tapped on the window. My heart was pounding! She looked startled, but rolled the window halfway down.

"Here," I said, lifting up Amber and tilting him in. He scrambled into her warm car. "He's your cat. He was yours first." My throat was tight, and my eyes started to prickle. "I guess I was… borrowing him."

Gretchen looked dumbfounded and said, "I don't know what to say."

My voice was all shaky. "Just say, 'Thank you.'" We looked at each other for what felt like a really long time, and I didn't know if I was doing the right thing or making the biggest mistake of my life. "If you go on any more trips, call us. We'll borrow him back and take really, really good care of him."

Amber settled onto Gretchen's lap, and I reached in and stroked his head. I studied him one last time, his mismatched ears and wispy whiskers and taco-colored fur. I even mumbled, "Good-bye, Taco." But he didn't look back at me. And to tell you the truth, my heart started breaking in two…then four…then a hundred little pieces.

"Thank you," Gretchen said, "Ava, thank you very much."

I was freezing. I hadn't put on my coat, and my nose and toes were tingling, and my hands were turning to ice, and my eyes were beginning to burn because I was beginning to cry. I didn't want to say, "You're welcome," and I didn't want to burst into tears, and it was too late to change my mind, so I just turned and ran home.

Inside, I shut the door behind me and went straight to Dad's big brown chair and curled up. And there, in front of Dad and Pip and Maybelle and even Zara, I started to bawl my eyes out. Big, loud, pitiful, wracking sobs. I couldn't help it.

The only one who didn't see me sobbing was Amber/Taco because he wasn't ours anymore. I'd given him away!

To be continued because I really have to pee.

Ava, Admirable but *Anguished*

2/2
A LITTLE LATER, IN MY PAJAMAS

Mom came home, and our living room was as sad as a cemetery. We told her everything, and she said, "Oh, honey," about twelve times and handed me tissues and even offered to be on the look-out for another cat, "not right away, not this week, but soon."

Zara kept saying she didn't get it. Maybelle just sat by me because she knew I felt miserable, and when you feel miserable, it helps if your best friend is with you even if she doesn't say a single solitary word.

After Zara and Maybelle left, we had dinner, and Pip barely said anything. I could tell she was really upset, and I felt bad because I hadn't thought about how much *she* loved Taco.

Now I'm going to bed. I hope I don't have nightmares.

A

2/3
IN THE LIBRARY

DEAR DIARY,

I'm skipping lunch and writing in you in the library. (I was afraid I might cry if I went to the lunchroom.)

I can't believe I gave Taco away! I guess I was trying to be noble or altruistic or mature or something, but really, I'm just a stupid moron. This morning Mom and Dad and Pip seemed depressed at breakfast. And of course Taco didn't come in and cheer us up and brush our legs and ask for *his* breakfast.

How could I have forgotten that even though Taco was mine, we *all* loved him?

Last night when I was trying to fall asleep, I could almost hear Taco padding into my room and almost feel him jumping onto my bed. I remembered a story from the Bible (not Aesop). It goes like this:

A bouncing baby boy was set before King Solomon, and two different women were crying and saying the baby was hers and that the other lady had stolen him. "It's my baby!" they both said. "She's lying!" King Solomon didn't know who was telling the truth, so he grabbed a sword and said, "Tell you what. Let's divide the baby in two, and you can each have half." The first lady said, "Okay, sounds fair," but the second lady started screaming bloody murder and said, "Noooo! Don't kill him! She can keep him! Just let him live!" And that's how King Solomon, who was very wise, knew the second lady was the real mother, and the first lady was a liar. He handed the baby back to his actual mom, and they lived happily ever after.

Here's what I think: Gretchen may have been Amber/Taco's first "mom," but I was his real "mom" too! Why oh why did I give him back??

Question: If I hadn't, would I have felt bad for Gretchen? Or guilty about keeping him?

Answer: Maybe. But not thaaat bad or guilty. Or maybe only at first?

Mr. Ramirez has been looking at me. I think he knows I'm upset. But he hasn't walked over because one of his rules is, "Never interrupt a person who is writing."

AVA THE IDIOT

2/3
AFTER DINNER

DEAR DIARY,

I came home after school, and even though I knew Taco wouldn't be there, I didn't know how it would feel.

Here's how it felt: awful.

Here's where Taco wasn't: He wasn't at the front door. He wasn't on Dad's brown chair. He wasn't on the armrest of the sofa. He wasn't by the fireplace. He wasn't hiding in Mom's closet. He wasn't on my bed. He wasn't anywhere.

Our house feels sad and silent and sorrowful. And more like a *house* than a *home*.

Dinner was pizza, but I could barely taste it. Mom started to tell a story about what happened at the clinic today, and some dog that had been peeing on the carpet and how the owners bought him "Tinkle Tonic." But then she stopped because she could tell none of us wanted to hear it.

AVA, CATLESS

2/4
MORNING

I didn't sleep well because the second I woke up, I remembered Taco was gone, and then I couldn't get back to sleep.

AVA, EXHAUSTED

2/4
AFTER SCHOOL

I don't know why I even opened you because I don't have anything to say.

You know the expression "at a loss for words"? That's me right now.

AVA, WORDLESS

2/4
BEDTIME

I noticed that Dad put a photo of Taco by his desk, Mom changed her cell phone photo to a picture of us with Taco, and Pip has been sketching more cats than flowers.

Dad, Mom, Pip, and I are very different, but loving Taco was one thing we all had in common.

A

2/5
AFTER SCHOOL

DEAR DIARY,

We had a spelling test and Chuck and I graded each other's papers and he said I'm amazing.

"I don't feel amazing," I said. "I feel sad." I told him I feel as sad as I felt on Tuesday.

"That's only three days ago," he said. "It would be weird if you didn't still feel sad." I nodded, and to be honest, that made me feel a tiny bit less sad.

Mrs. Lemons asked if I was okay. I shrugged because I couldn't bear to tell her about Taco, and besides, I was pretty sure Zara already had.

"Ava, you'll like this," Mrs. Lemons said, and wrote this on the board:

"I love cooking
my pets and
my family."

She asked our class, "What's wrong with this sentence?"

Well, I could have blurted, "It needs commas!" because on the board, it looked like the confession of a cannibal.

But I let Riley answer because I didn't want to talk about pets or family.

After school, Dad said he wanted to try a recipe for "spaghetti and wheat balls."

I said, "Please don't," and (this is embarrassing) my voice got wobbly. Dad hugged me, and I started crying a little.

He said he'd make me regular bow tie noodles, and I nodded into his chest, which got the front of his shirt damp.

Observation: When you feel sad, you want regular food, not fancy food or experimental food. Right now, if Jerry Valentino told me to write about something "warm and comforting," I might even write about bow tie noodles.

I wish I'd never written "The Cat Who Wouldn't Purr"!

Except…wait.

You know what?

That's not totally true.

Confession: (1) I liked writing it, and (2) I liked that people liked reading it.

I guess what I wish is that Gretchen Guthrie had never seen Taco's photo in the newspaper. I can't believe I gave her back her cat—*our* cat.

She loves him, that's true, but I love him too. *Loved?*

I wonder how Taco/Amber is doing.

Here's how I'm doing: bad.

A

2/5
AFTER DINNER

DEAR DIARY,

I decided I had to *do something*, so I got out a piece of paper and wrote Gretchen a letter. After a few false starts and one really long, dumb practice letter, I finally settled with:

> Dear Gretchen Guthrie,
> I've been thinking about you and Amber (a.k.a. Taco). Can you tell him I say hi? And that my whole family misses him a lot?
> Please write back. And please send a photo that I can frame. It doesn't have to be new, but if possible, I would like it to be of him as a cat, not a kitten, because that's how I will always think of him.
>
> Thank you.
> Ava Wren

I was going to draw a cat next to my name, but instead, I folded up my letter and tucked it into an envelope. Then I knocked on

Pip's door and asked her to draw Taco on the back. She did. I added a cat sticker on the front and knocked on Mom and Dad's door. Mom took my decorated envelope and said she'd look up Gretchen's address and mail the letter this weekend.

A

2/6
Saturday Morning, Still in Bed

I dreamed we got a big friendly golden retriever. He fetched sticks and chased balls and went on walks and seemed like he would never leave our side! But then he went swimming in a dark pond, and he came out and started shaking off the water. He was shaking and shaking, and suddenly he started fading away and disappearing! I tried to hug him, but he wasn't there.

I woke up crying! And now I'm the exact *opposite* of well rested.

A

2/6
Saturday Afternoon

Dear Diary,

Dad is rereading a giant book called *War and Peace.* He says he "can't put it down." It's so long and heavy, I don't know how he can pick it *up*!

He said he wishes he spoke Russian because it "probably lost something in translation."

I said, "Do books ever *gain* something in translation?"

He laughed and said he was going to have to think about that.

I was glad I made Dad laugh. And I wished I liked to read more because then I could be all involved in someone else's up-and-down life instead of just my own.

But I'm more of a writer than a reader. So far, anyway.

How long will it be until I feel better? I'm glad I have you.

Ava, Still Moping

2/6
AFTER DINNER

DEAR DIARY,

Pip drove me crazy tonight. Every fifteen minutes, she said things like, "It's vanilla, but it's not chocolate."

Or "It's good, but it's not great."

Or "It's silly, but it's not clever."

Or "It's funny, but it's not amusing."

Or "It's terrible, but it's not awful."

Or "It's noodles, but it's not pasta."

Or "It's speedy, but it's not fast."

Finally I told her I didn't know what she was talking about and I was going to clobber her if she didn't cut it out. She said, "It's clobber, but it's not hit, *and* it's killing, but it's not murdering." Well, somehow, just like that, I figured out that she was doing a word game about double letters.

So I said, "It's le*tt*ers, but it's not sounds, right?"

"That is ind*ee*d co*rr*ect!" she said.

Not to be violent, but considering the gl*oo*my m*oo*d I've been in, Pip is lucky I didn't hack her up into i*tt*y bi*tt*y pieces.

AVA E*LL*E WREN, NOT IN THE M*OO*D

P.S. I'm probably lucky Pip is even talking to me. If she'd given away our family's first real pet, I'd have a hard time forgiving her. Sometimes I do stuff that's well-meaning but boneheaded. Dad said that I'm "a little impulsive," which I think means "not thinking enough."

2/7
Sunday at 2

I asked Maybelle to come over and said she could even invite Zara if she wanted. I need to get out of my funk. These have been the longest days of my life. They've been like *forty-eight*-hour days!!

Ava, Trying

2/7
AFTER DINNER

DEAR DIARY,

Wait. Till. You. Hear. This.

Mom and Dad were running an errand, and Maybelle and Zara and Pip were playing Monopoly, and I was under a blanket on the sofa.

After her turn, Zara got up and peeked out the window. "You guys," she said, "isn't that Q-tip Lady's car?"

Maybelle and Zara and Pip smooshed against the window.

"It *is*! What the heck does she want now?" Zara said.

"Maybe to pay us for the vet bills?" Pip said.

"Why isn't she getting out?" Maybelle said.

"Yeah. Why is she just *sitting* there? It's like she's *thinking* about getting out." Zara kept narrating, so I went to look. "She opened the door but then she closed it again!" Zara made a face. "Wait, now she *is* getting out—but she's still taking her time about it!"

Maybelle said, "Should we go to her?"

Zara said, "No way!" so we all just watched as Gretchen started heading up our front walk.

"Here she comes," Pip said.

The doorbell rang, and we looked at each other, and I decided I'd be the one to let her in.

Well, get ready because here comes the Holy Moly part: Gretchen stepped inside, and instead of handing us a check, she unbuttoned her red coat. First, I heard a muffled mew. Next, I saw a furry snout. Then I saw soft whiskers and green eyes. And finally there was Taco/Amber!!!! Gretchen held him out (her eyes were a little puffy), and I stretched out my arms, and she pressed him against me, and I closed my arms around him, and she backed away. And Taco peered up at me as if to say, "Hi."

"Ava," Gretchen began, "I love this cat. I really do. But I've hardly slept a wink all week, and Amber didn't sleep through the nights either—"

"Me neither," I said although I hadn't meant to interrupt.

"I think he's been sleeping all day while I'm at work. At night, he's been running around and meowing and"—she looked at me—"asking about you."

Was she saying what I hoped she was saying?

"Ava," Gretchen continued, "I work long hours and I travel a lot for business. Even this week, I'll be away three days." She sighed. "I guess I've come to realize that I'm not around as much for…our cat as you and your family would be."

I kept petting Taco and listening as hard as I could. I could feel Pip and Maybelle and Zara staring at me, but I didn't want to look away from Taco and Gretchen.

"What I'm saying is: I'm glad he found a good home when he needed one, and that you love him as much as I do. So if you want to keep him, well, I want you to." Her voice quavered. "I know you'll take good care of him."

I held Taco tight—he was the softest, sweetest, furriest feline in the world. "For real?" I squeaked. "You're giving him back?" I wanted to be 100 percent sure before I let myself do a happy dance, even in my head.

She nodded, and I hugged Taco harder—but still gently, of course. "Yes. But if you let me, I *would* like to visit him from time to time."

Zara lunged forward and gave Gretchen a big hug. "I'm sorry I lied and said he died," she said. "Sometimes I just say stuff."

Gretchen smiled. "You were trying to help your friend."

Zara looked at me and I realized it was true, she was. Even when Zara bugged me, like when we were making paper mice, or when she talked to Chuck, or when she told Mr. Ramirez about our fish book, maybe, in her own way, she was trying to be helpful. And I couldn't really blame her for wanting to be friends with Maybelle.

Pip, Maybelle, and Zara all started petting Taco, who was still in my arms. Pip turned to Gretchen and said, "You can visit him anytime. Just call. And if you ever want to, we could go with you to the rescue center and help you pick out a new kitten."

"They have really cute ones," I said.

"You could even get a *pair* of kittens," Pip said. "That way, they could keep each other company during the day, chasing each other around and tiring each other out."

"If you take *two* kittens, it's free," I added.

Gretchen smiled at us both. "Let's take one day at a time." She buttoned her red coat back up. "Please tell your parents that I would like to stop by from time to time," she said. "And tell them they raised two very good kids."

Well, we were thanking her and saying one last good-bye, when guess who came home? Mom and Dad!

We told them everything, and they thanked Gretchen too. After a little while, Dad suddenly said, "Would you like to stay for dinner? We're having Irish stew. It's one of my signature dishes."

She hesitated for two seconds, then said, "You know what? I'd like that very much."

Dad said, "Great," so I asked if Maybelle and Zara could stay too. He said, "Sure." Maybelle called her parents, Zara called her grandparents, and Mom and Pip and I set the table for seven. We even lit candles, which we hardly ever do. And we all had a really nice dinner, grown-ups at one end, and Pip, Maybelle, Zara, and I at the other. It felt a tiny bit like Thanksgiving, but without the turkey and cranberries and stress.

We talked about a lot of things, and I asked Gretchen if she got my letter. She said no, and Mom said, "That's because I just mailed it. There's no mail on Sunday." Gretchen said she'd keep an eye out for it, and Pip mentioned that she drew a picture of Taco on the back.

Speaking of Taco, he stayed close by all during dinner. He was curled up on the sofa, fast asleep, one white paw over his face.

And I have to say: he looked right at home.

Ava Wren, Happy Again

2/7
BEDTIME

DEAR DIARY,

I was looking over these pages when Dad knocked on my door. "Come in," I said, halfway under the covers.

"Special delivery," Dad said and deposited Taco on my lap.

"Thank you!" I said.

"Can you believe how everything worked out?"

I nodded but didn't answer because I didn't want to scare Taco.

"You know," Dad said, "not to play the Homonym Game or anything, but, Ava, you did the *write* thing and the *right* thing."

"Last year, I did the write thing and the *wrong* thing," I whispered. It was always embarrassing to remember that I'd based "Sting of the Queen Bee" on our friend Bea.

"Well, tonight I think you should feel proud of yourself."

"You know how you and I are *both* writers?" I replied.

"Yes," he said and smiled.

"Someday I might want to write a book about a girl and a cat."

"Why not?" he said, a little too loudly.

I said "Shhh" and pointed to Taco. He was settling in by my shoulder, and for once, he was facing my face, not my feet.

"Someday," Dad said, lowering his voice, "I can see you writing that book. But right now, it's time to turn off the light." He gave me a good-night kiss and gave Taco a good-night pat.

"Dad," I said, showing him you, my diary. "Can you believe I'm almost out of pages?"

"Impressive! Maybe we can go to Bates Books tomorrow and get you a new one."

"Okay if I write for a few more minutes?"

"Okay by me," he said and left the door open a crack.

What I want to do now is scribble down a few notes for the book I might want to write someday. It could be about a girl who rescues a cat and doesn't know that the cat has *already* been rescued. When she finds out, she's very upset but also pretty mature for someone who just turned eleven, and she ends up offering the cat back to his first owner even though this makes her cry her eyes out. (She's not thaaaat mature.) Five days later, the first owner says the girl can keep the cat after all. So the story has a happy ending, which is good, since it would be for kids.

Mom just came in to say good night. She saw Taco and whispered, "Sweet dreams, Ava. You too, Taco."

I whispered, "You too, Mom."

I've been thinking. If my story were a fable, it would need a moral. Maybe something like: When you're generous, it comes back to you.

I wonder if that is true. I bet it usually is.

I also wonder how long it would take to write an *entire* book.

Rhymes and haiku (and sometimes rhyming haiku) come to me pretty fast. For instance:

I like my cat and

I like to write, but now it's

time to say good night.

But a book? That would be a *lot* of work. Then again, it might be fun work—especially if I use my head and my heart and my senses.

Well, I'm going to turn off the light. I'm also going to try *not* to move a single solitary muscle—even if I get an itch—because I want Taco to stay with me as long as possible. Right now his eyes are closed, and he's purring *and* kneading. It's like he's in a trance.

I love him so much! And he loves me back—in his own skittish, cattish way.

Will he stay with me until morning? I doubt it. But I hope that tonight at least, he'll stick around long enough for me to fall asleep first.

Even if he doesn't, Taco is my *forever* cat—I'm never letting him go again!

I love the sound of his purring and purring.

What a purrfect way to end this day!

H-U-H. Maybe it's a good way to end a book too...

PALINDROMES AND BONUS PALINDROMES

How many palindromes and palindrome sentences are there? Tons! Especially if you look at other languages.

In Spanish, there's *YO SOY*, which means "I am," and *LA RUTA NATURAL*, which means "the natural route," and *ANITA LAVA LA TINA*, which means "Anita washes the tub."

In French, there's *ÉTÉ*, which is "summer," and *ÉSOPE RESTE ICI ET SE REPOSE,* which, believe it or not, means "Aesop stays here and rests."

And that's just for starters!

A total stickler might argue that true palindromes cannot have commas or colons or periods or apostrophes or accents. But Ava Wren is more of a word nerd than a stickler. And while she likes one-word palindromes, such as KOOK and BOOB and ROTATOR and REDIVIDER (not to mention WOW, XOX, YAY, and ZZZ), she loves longer ones.

Here are some of Ava's favorites, old and new, in alphabetical order:

ABLE WAS I ERE I SAW ELBA.

A DOG! A PANIC IN A PAGODA!

A MAN, A PLAN, A CANAL: PANAMA
A NUT FOR A JAR OF TUNA
A SANTA AT NASA!
A SANTA LIVED AS A DEVIL AT NASA.
AS I PEE, SIR, I SEE PISA!
A TOYOTA'S A TOYOTA
BORROW OR ROB
CAIN: A MANIAC
DENNIS SINNED.
DESSERTS, I STRESSED!
DID I DO, O GOD, DID I AS I SAID I'D DO? GOOD, I DID!
DOG DOO? GOOD GOD!
DO GEESE SEE GOD?
DRAWN ONWARD
DRAW, O COWARD!
DUMB MOBS BOMB MUD.
DUMB MUD
ED IS ON NO SIDE.
EVA, CAN I STAB BATS IN A CAVE?
EVADE ME, DAVE!
EVIL OLIVE
FLEE TO ME, REMOTE ELF!
FUN ENUF
GNU DUNG
GO HANG A SALAMI, I'M A LASAGNA HOG!
GOLD LOG
HE DID, EH?
HE LIVED AS A DEVIL, EH?
HE WON A TOYOTA NOW, EH?
HOHOHOH
I DID, DID I?
I'M, ALAS, A SALAMI.
I MOAN, NAOMI!
IN WORDS, ALAS, DROWN I.
I PREFER PI.
LION IN OIL
LIVE NOT ON EVIL!
LLAMA MALL
LONELY TYLENOL
MA IS AS SELFLESS AS I AM.
MADAM, I'M ADAM.

MADAM, IN EDEN I'M ADAM.
MIRROR RIM
MY GYM
NIAGARA, O ROAR AGAIN!
NAME NOW ONE MAN.
NEIL, AN ALIEN!
NEVER ODD OR EVEN.
NO, IT IS OPPOSITION.
NO MELON, NO LEMON
NO MISS, IT IS SIMON.
NORMA IS AS SELFLESS AS I AM, RON.
NO SIR—AWAY! A PAPAYA WAR IS ON!
NO SIR, PREFER PRISON!
NOT A BANANA BATON!
NOT A TON
NOT SO, BOSTON!
NOW EVE, WE'RE HERE, WE'VE WON.
NOW I WON!
NOW SIR, A WAR IS WON.
NURSES RUN.
OH WHO WAS IT I SAW, OH WHO?
PARTY BOOBYTRAP
POP POP POP
REWARD DRAWER
RISE TO VOTE, SIR!
ROY, AM I MAYOR?
SENILE FELINES
SH! TOM SEES MOTHS.
SIR, I'M IRIS.
SO MANY DYNAMOS!
SOME MEN INTERPRET NINE MEMOS.
SPACE CAPS
STACK CATS
STAR RATS
STAR COMEDY BY DEMOCRATS!
STELLA WON NO WALLETS.
STEP ON NO PETS.
SUE US.
TATTARRATTAT
TOO BAD I HID A BOOT.
TOP SPOT
TOO HOT TO HOOT
WAS IT A CAR OR A CAT I SAW?
WONTON? NOT NOW.

YO BANANA BOY!
and
#AMMIT I'M MAD

Oh wait, here's one more:
AIBOHPHOBIA
It means the irrational fear of palindromes!

Acknowledgments

Ava fills her diary without even thinking, but me, I work hard on these pages. Fortunately, I have family, friends, and pros who offer ideas and enthusiasm, as well as coffee and chocolate.

I am beyond grateful to my daughters Emme and Lizzi and my husband Rob Ackerman, as well as to Eric, Cynthia, and Marybeth Weston, Linda Richichi, and cousins Matt Bird and Bonnie Beer.

Sam Forman helped me get unstuck, and when I changed Zara's name, he talked me into changing it back. Maybelle Keyser-Butson and Denver Butson and Kathy and H-A-N-N-A-H Lathen helped me dig deeper. Karolina Ksiazek was there at the start and finish. Dwight Edwards and Linda Jones (Gotham Veterinary Center), Celia Aidinoff, and the Ezells all shared pet care insights. Thanks too to Paula and Cara Raskin, Kiera Little, Suzannah Weiss, Barb Doran, H-A-N-N-A-H Judy, Katherine Dye, and Jennifer Lu, as well as to students at Maret, Clairbourne, John Thomas Dye, Columbus School for Girls, P.S. 183 in Manhattan, and P.S. 15 in Brooklyn, who listened to the first pages. And a high five to Elizabeth Winthrop, who encouraged me early on to let Ava have her way with words.

At lunch in April 2013, I met my wonderful editor, Steve Geck, and we realized that he and I and publicist Derry Wilkens had all adopted our cats from Petco. W-O-W. Turns out book jacket artist Victoria Jamieson also adopted her cat from Petco! Here's to adoption events and animal shelters and caregivers everywhere.

I also want to thank Heather Moore, Valerie Pierce, Heidi Weiland, Jillian Bergsma, Rachel Gilmer, Sabrina Baskey, Katie Anderson, Elizabeth Boyer, Alex Yeadon, Kate Prosswimmer, Dominique Raccah, and the whole Sourcebooks Jabberwocky team.

I'm thrilled to be represented by the amazing Susan Ginsburg (and Stacy Testa) of Writers House. And here's to Middlebury College and the New York Society Library, where I have used prompts to teach writing, and to Ragdale Foundation where I have written and rewritten and rewritten. (An extra-special thank-you to my J-term students.)

Finally, one last shout-out to furry, feisty Mike the Muse, who is affectionate on his own terms and will probably never spend an entire night in one place.

Find out what happens next in

2/8
BEFORE DINNER

DEAR NEW DIARY,

I'm pretty upset about what happened today.

My new friend Zara asked if I'd heard about Chuck.

"No, what about him?" I said.

"He and Kelli are going out," she said.

"How do you know?" I asked because this did *not* seem possible, and, well, Zara has kind of a big mouth.

She said Chuck was on the bus minding his own business when Kelli hopped on and sat right next to him without asking. She was wearing one of her sparkly headbands—she has about a million—and sneaking bites of banana bread even though you're not supposed to eat on the bus. She offered him a piece. And he took it.

Later, in homeroom, Kelli passed Chuck a note that said, "Do you want to go out?" Zara said it had two circles, one marked YES and one marked NO. At first Chuck didn't answer, but Kelli made a sad puppy face, so he put an X in the YES circle and passed it back.

And now they are "going out"!!

I have to say, this really bugs me.

Number one: we're only in fifth grade.

Number two: Chuck and I have been friends since the apple-picking field trip in kindergarten, and Kelli just moved here last year, and I've never once noticed him notice her.

It just doesn't seem right that they've said about five sentences to each other—total—and all of a sudden they're "going out"! How long has she even liked him? Did she start *today*?

And how can they be going out when none of us is allowed to go anywhere anyway?

Lunch was spaghetti and meatballs, which I usually love, but my insides felt like cold, stuck-together spaghetti. It didn't help that Zara and my best friend Maybelle were talking about Valentine's Day, which is Saturday.

Our grade has three Emilys, but only one Ava, one Maybelle, and one Zara, and lately the six of us have been sitting together at lunch. Well, it's usually all-girl or all-boy, but today, Kelli plunked her tray down at Chuck's table! I was in shock! The Emilys just giggled, and Emily Jenkins said, "Kelli and Chuck make a good couple." And everyone agreed!

I swear, that made me want to throw up my meatballs. (Sorry if that's gross.)

The problem is that I'm not supposed to care as much as I guess I do. Last month, Zara asked if I liked Chuck, and I said no.

Why *do* I care anyway? Chuck is sweet and funny, but I think of him as a brother.

At least I *think* I think of him as a brother.

A sweet, funny brother.

Nothing more.

We're just friends.

H-U-H. That's a weird expression, isn't it? "*Just* friends." As though years of being friends is less important than *hours* of "going out."

AVA, ANNOYED

2/8
BEDTIME

DEAR DIARY,

One thing about Kelli: she's bubbly. Very bubbly. If you poured too much bubble bath in your bathtub and forgot to turn off the water, that's how much she bubbles. She's always laughing hysterically as if the whole world is a joke and she's the only one who gets it.

She also does splits and handstands and cartwheels at random times, which is impressive but show-offy. And she talks a lot about her lake house and vacations, which isn't polite considering the rest of us have one house, not two, and we have "staycations," not fancy trips. Another thing that bothers me is when Kelli's headband and fingernail polish match. (Today, they were emerald.)

She should take it down a notch.

Or move to a different school!

Anyway, when I got home today, Dad was taking out ingredients to make a yucky, squishy squash recipe for Meatless Monday (his new-ish tradition), so I told him a vegetable riddle:

Question: What room has no windows or doors?

Answer: A mushroom!

I asked if we could go to Bates Books so I could get a new diary—you!—and he said sure. (Dad likes that we're both writers.) I was glad because I *really* needed a place to dump all my feelings—as you can see because I've *already* filled five pages!

So far in my life, I have finished two diaries and given up on six. The unfinished ones are in a dead diary graveyard underneath my underwear.

I got my coat, and we drove over, and Dad and I walked inside the bookstore, and there were hearts everywhere! Red ones and pink ones. Big ones and little ones. Flat ones and 3-D ones and ones hanging from the ceiling. There were also Valentine's Day books, cards, pins, pens, mugs, magnets, stickers, and even giant heart doilies and heart-shaped boxes of chocolate. The owners of the bookstore are my friend Bea's parents, and she says they try to sell tons of holiday knickknacks so they can afford to keep selling regular books.

Confession: the happy hearts made me sort of sad.

I just can't believe Kelli asked Chuck out! And that this aggravates me so much.

Dad offered to buy me a box of Valentine cards, but I said no thanks. I told him that in second and third grade, our whole class used to exchange valentines, but now I'm too old.

"Too old?" Dad thought that was funnier than my mushroom riddle. "How about chocolate kisses? Are you too old for chocolate kisses?" He picked up a bag of chocolate kisses wrapped in silver and set it on the counter. Fortunately, moods are contagious, and Dad's good mood was helping me shake off my bad mood.

"I am the exact right age for chocolate kisses," I said, and on the way home, I unwrapped one for each of us.

AVA, AGGRAVATED

2/9
EARLY MORNING

Dear Diary,

I just had the worst nightmare! I dreamed I was naked in school!! NAKED IN SCHOOL!!! I was in gym class and looked down and I wasn't wearing any clothes at all.

Not even any underwear!

Not even a…fig leaf! (That's what Adam and E-V-E wore.)

In my dream, I went racing full speed to the locker room and hid behind a shower curtain and held on tight. When I woke up, I was holding on to my *sheets* for dear life. And that's when I realized it was just a dream.

Phew!!

I think I had that dream because our gym teacher, Mrs. Kocivar, said that next year in sixth grade, girls can shower in school if they want to.

I will *never* want to!

Ava, Who Prefers Privacy

P.S. Mrs. Kocivar also showed us some modern dance steps and said we should watch Kelli because she was doing it "perfectly." I made a little face and looked around to see if anyone else wanted to make a face back, but no one did. Am I the only person who doesn't think Kelli is perfectly perfect??

2/9
AFTER SCHOOL

DEAR DIARY,

Guess who I just ran into? Chuck!

Dad had to run some errands, so I went along. At the bank, I heard a crazy clinking clanking sound. I turned and there was Chuck pouring a bagful of pennies, nickels, dimes, and quarters into a giant sorting machine. When I went to say hi, it felt like my heart was beating as loudly as the machine. Which surprised me.

Since when do I feel nervous around Chuck?

Chuck said his mom said he could keep all the coins he found in their house and added, "But I bet she had *no* idea how many I would find!" He said he looked in pockets and drawers and under cushions and everywhere.

We waited together while the numbers kept going up, up, up. When they finally stopped, you know what the total was? $18.17!

"You're rich!" I teased. "What are you going to do with all that money?"

"I don't know."

"You could buy me bubblemint gum!"

He laughed and asked what my dad had cooked for "Barfy Monday." I told him squishy squash and made it sound extra gross, and then I was tempted to ask about his new girlfriend, but his mom came over and said they had to go. His mom always makes me nervous, probably because she is very tall and serious and has excellent posture.

Chuck is tall too, but he never used to make me nervous. He just made me laugh. While we were waiting for the noisy machine to count his money, for instance, he told me a joke that had a word from last Friday's spelling test: "Two *cannibals* were eating a clown, and one said to the other, 'Does this taste funny to you?'" (Hehe.)

I was glad he told it because it made things seem normal-ish between us even though I feel like they aren't.

Back home, our kitchen smelled scrumptious. Pip was baking gingerbread men (and gingerbread women and teens and kids and babies) with a seventh-grade girl named Tanya. Pip hardly ever has friends over, and I'd never met Tanya. Dad went upstairs, and I reached for a chocolate kiss, but the bowl was empty. I was about to say, "Pip, you ate *all* the chocolate kisses?!" when I realized Tanya must have helped.

If I had to describe Tanya, I guess I'd say that she is *pretty* but also *pretty* heavy. I've never really thought of this before, but Pip might be the smallest kid in seventh grade, and Tanya might be the… opposite?? It feels weird to write this down, and I don't mean that she's just a little chubby and who even cares? I mean that when she has checkups, I bet her doctor talks to her about weight and stuff.

Anyway, Tanya said that when she met our cat, she felt like she "already knew him" because of my story in the *Misty Oaks Monitor*, "The Cat Who Wouldn't Purr," which she'd "really liked."

"When did you adopt Taco Cat?"

"He was my birthday present on January 1 when I turned eleven."

She showed me two pencil sketches she'd made of him. They were both cute, and she'd even drawn in the white zigzag on his forehead and the white tip of his tail.

"You can have one," she said.

"Really?" I asked.

"Really."

I picked one and just now taped it on the rim of my mirror.

Hey, M-I-R-R-O-R-R-I-M is a palindrome! Which is funny because palindromes are sort of like words in mirrors since they're the same backward and forward.

I've never thought of M-I-R-R-O-R-R-I-M before, and trust me, I, A-V-A, sister of P-I-P, daughter of A-N-N-A and B-O-B, and owner of T-A-C-O-C-A-T, have thought of piles of palindromes.

Well, I helped Pip and Tanya take their gingerbread families out of the oven, and we let them cool. Then, minutes later, we started nibbling them, feet first, as though *we* were cannibals. Suddenly Pip said, "Whoa! We'd better save a few!" I think she realized it would have been bad if M-O-M or D-A-D walked into a yummy-smelling kitchen and found only ginger crumbs instead of ginger people.

After Tanya left, Pip told me that they were supposed to

have started their art project for Spanish but instead started baking and cutting out pastel hearts for a Valentine collage for Pip's boyfriend.

Sometimes I can hardly believe that Pip, who used to be so shy, has a real live valentine. And that he's *B*en *B*ates, *B*ea's *B*ig *B*rother (*al*literation *al*ert).

I can't imagine having a valentine.

(Or can I??)

Ava, Ambivalent (that's when you're not sure)

2/10
BEFORE DINNER

DEAR DIARY,

Fifth grade is more complicated than fourth grade. Not just the math. *Everything*. It used to be that Maybelle was my best friend, and Chuck was my best guy friend, and that was that. Now Maybelle hangs out with Zara, and Chuck hangs out with Kelli, and I'm supposed to be okay with it all.

Even gym is complicated because some girls are "developing" and some aren't (like me). I think everyone is a little freaked out. The "mature" kids whose bodies are changing, and the other kids whose bodies are just sitting there. (Or standing or walking or running or whatever.)

Tomorrow we're starting a new class called FLASH. It stands for *F*amily *L*ife *A*nd *S*ocial *H*ealth. The funny thing is that our health teacher's name is Ms. *Sick*le. (Get it?)

It meets every Thursday.

My favorite class, of course, is English. Today Mrs. Lemons showed us something she'd printed from the Internet:

1 2 3 4 5 6 7 8 9 10 11 12 13 14 15

Re-post when you find the mitsake.

I kept looking and looking and was about to say, "I don't see any mistake" when I noticed it was a *spelling* "mitsake"—not a numbers one!

After class, Chuck and I started walking out the door together, the way we always used to, but there was Kelli waiting for him on the other side! I couldn't believe she came to meet him!! You might call that friendly, but I call it stalker-y! (Not that stalkers usually wear sparkly headbands.)

Chuck walked off with Kelli, and Zara looked at me like she could tell I was mad and sad.

Which I was.

Both.

I even mumbled, "I don't get what Chuck sees in her."

Without waiting a *s*ingle *s*olitary *s*econd, Zara said, "Well, she is pretty. And she's popular."

Popular? I've never really thought about popularity. Or maybe I thought popularity was something we didn't *have* to think about until puberty, which is something else I don't like to think about.

"And she's a good dancer," Zara continued. "And she's good at sports. And—"

Was Zara just getting warmed up? I put my hand in the air as if to say, "Stop!" Then I mentioned that in the girls' room, Kelli had applied lip gloss and announced that she likes "the natural look," and I'd wanted to say, "If you want to look natural, why wear makeup at all?"

Zara laughed, so I added, "I just hope Chuck doesn't get his feelings hurt."

Zara looked at me sideways as though she wasn't one hundred percent convinced this was my biggest concern.

Ava, Concerned

Have you read

AVA AND PIP

Carol Weston

Two sisters were never so different.

Meet outgoing Ava Wren, a fun fifth grader who feels invisible in her own family and whose big sister is very shy. When Pip's thirteenth birthday turns into a disaster, Ava gets a story idea for a library contest.

But uh-oh, Ava should never have written "Sting of the Queen Bee." Can Ava get out of the mess she has made? Can she help Pip find her voice—and maybe even find her own?

About the Author

Carol Weston lives in Manhattan. Her parents were word nerds in the best way, and Carol kept diaries as a girl. Her sixteen books include *Ava and Pip*, *Ava and Taco Cat*, *Ava XOX*, *The Speed of Life*, and four Melanie Martin diary novels as well as *Girltalk: All the Stuff Your Sister Never Told You*, which was translated into twelve languages. The *New York Times* called *Ava and Pip* "a love letter to language." Carol lives in Manhattan. For info and videos, visit carolweston.com.